WE WEREN'T LOOKING TO BE FOUND

WE WEREN'T LOOKING TO BE FOUND

STEPHANIE KUEHN

HYPERION
Los Angeles   New York

CONTENT WARNING:
Please be aware that this book explores issues
of substance abuse, suicide, and self-harm.

First Edition, June 2022
10 9 8 7 6 5 4 3 2 1
FAC-020093-22126
Printed in the United States

This book is set in Georgia/Microsoft
Designed by Zareen Johnson

Library of Congress Cataloging-in-Publication Data
Names: Kuehn, Stephanie, author.
Title: We weren't looking to be found / Stephanie Kuehn.
Other titles: We were not looking to be found
Description: First edition. • Los Angeles ; New York : Hyperion, 2022. •
Audience: Ages 14–18. • Audience: Grades 10–12. • Summary: "Two girls
find friendship on their path to mental health in a story of acceptance,
recovery, and resilience"— Provided by publisher.
Identifiers: LCCN 2021037392 • ISBN 9781368064101 (hardcover) •
ISBN 9781368066747 (ebook)
Subjects: CYAC: Psychiatric hospitals—Fiction. • Substance abuse—Fiction.
• Self-mutilation—Fiction. • African Americans—Fiction. •
Hispanic Americans—Fiction. • LCGFT: Novels.
Classification: LCC PZ7.K94872 We 2022 • DDC [Fic]—dc23
LC record available at https://lccn.loc.gov/2021037392

Reinforced binding

Visit www.hyperionteens.com

For my mother and for Tessa,
the best women I know.

Peach Tree Hills Treatment Facility
Peach Tree Hills, GA

CAMILA

THE THOUGHTS SWIRLING through my head at the moment are not nice ones. They're ones like: *I want to strangle her.* And: *I'm definitely telling staff about those pills she's hiding.* And also: *I'm not doing anything for anyone else ever again.*

Occam's razor would say the reason I'm having these thoughts is because I'm not a nice person. I'm inclined to agree, although Dr. R, in all her glass-half-full optimism, would probably counter with something like *That's just your depression talking, Camila,* or *What's another possibility that you can come up with?* since it's sort of her job to try and make me not hate myself. But that isn't even my concern at the moment, since the person I hate more than anything right now is my roommate, Dani.

I'm not sure she realizes this.

Dani and I are currently walking side by side—two brown-skinned girls marching in tandem across Peach Tree Hills' perfectly manicured lawn, both heading toward the locked storage building on the far end of the property. But don't mistake our closeness for intimacy; we're doing this because we have to. The glossy brochures might describe this place as "a holistically minded treatment facility for adolescent girls located in the scenic foothills of Georgia's Blue Ridge Mountains," but that's all a fancy way of saying it's a prison that's got country club taste.

I do take some of the blame for our present situation. Okay, most of it, actually. Approximately twenty-four hours have passed since I broke us out of here, and only eighteen since we were caught and hauled back. Our punishment is to clean out the storage room, and it's no doubt meant to be a lesson, too. But none of this is the source of my present anger. My simmering rage. No, being held accountable for something I absolutely did is one thing.

Betrayal is another.

"Hurry up." Dani forges ahead on legs far longer than my own. My dancer's heart flares with envy at the sight, and I don't bother tamping it down. "Might as well get it over with."

"Easy for you to say," I snarl.

Dani whirls to face me, her Bambi-brown eyes wide with feigned innocence. "What's that supposed to mean?"

"*What's that supposed to mean?*" Caustic, fiery, I mock her rich-girl baby voice, twisting it into something that sounds like a mash-up of a lesser Kardashian and Kellyanne Conway.

Those Bambi eyes narrow. "Seriously?"

I fold my arms. Refuse to answer.

Dani snorts. "Real mature, Cams."

We approach the outbuilding, and a part of me wants to make a break for it—just throw a leg over the property fence and take off running. It wouldn't get me anywhere, though. Just lost. Tired. Maybe mauled by a bear. Although, with my luck, I'd probably end up at the bottom of a ravine with nothing to show for it but a few broken bones and a lot of suffering. But it wouldn't be the kind of suffering that matters.

The kind I long for.

The key chain rattles as Dani pulls it from her pocket. I hang back, hands shoved into the pockets of my cutoffs, and watch as she fumbles with the door. The lock's sticky—the whole frame's warped from the Georgia heat—and it takes a few tries, but the door opens at last, pushing inward with a groan.

Curiosity inches me forward, beating back my ire until I'm huddled beside Dani. We crouch on the threshold, peering inward.

"What *is* this place?" she asks in a hushed tone.

I point to the faded sign pinned to the door itself:

PEACH TREE HILLS
LOST AND FOUND

With a bob of her head, Dani steps in, and I follow. The space is larger than I expected, more echoey meeting hall than storage closet, and it stretches as far as I can see.

A mustiness hangs in the air; shadows linger in every corner. The only light is natural light, a muted midday sun pouring in through casement windows that run along the upper perimeter of the room and illuminate row after row of modular shelving lined from floor to ceiling. Something in the stillness and the silence offers up the impression we've entered a library of sorts, a place cavernous, rare, and worthy of reverence.

"What're we supposed to do?" I ask.

"I'm not sure."

"Well, we can't possibly go through all these shelves. Not in a day. Or even a year."

"No," Dani agrees. "We can't."

She reaches for a plastic bin that sits on the nearest shelf and pulls it toward her. I spy a name scrawled on the front with Sharpie: *Amelia D.*

With care and caution Dani pours Amelia's belongings onto the floor, but it still hurts to witness. Nothing breaks or shatters, yet there's sorrow in seeing someone else's past reduced to junk, even if that's all it is. The items Amelia D. left behind include two shoes—a broken flip-flop and a dusty loafer—some faded garments that have been folded and tucked neatly into a sealed Ziploc bag, and a framed photograph of a blond-haired male toddler holding a puppy. This last item I scoop up and I quickly run my finger across the boy's face, sweeping off dust.

Dani moves on to the next row of shelves. The bins are larger, and they aren't marked with any names, although some attempt's been made at organization. An entire shelf is dedicated to clothing, another for personal items, another for electronics. She riffles through a few before pausing. "Wait, I'm confused. If they actually know who some of these items belong to, why haven't they sent them back?"

Why indeed? I look up from the photograph, and I can see the moment it hits her. The moment she realizes it's not only items that can be lost and never found.

"Oh, Cams." She turns and throws her arms around me. "I'm so sorry."

"Don't be." I stiffen beneath her touch.

"You know why I had to tell them, don't you?" Dani murmurs as I inhale the warm scent of her hair, her skin. As I focus my attention on anything other than what she's actually saying. "You know I only want you to get better."

Do I?

"What's this?" I ask. She still clings to me, but something's come between us. Literally. It's pressing into my chest.

Dani reaches to pull out an item I didn't realize she was holding, and I gasp to see it's a *music box*. An intricate one, carved from dark wood and painted with rich colors. I stare, transfixed.

The dancer perched on top isn't your stereotypical pale-faced ballerina in her perfect pink pointe shoes. She's different. Her shoes are ruby red, and her dress flares from her hips in a flash of black and gold. She's got her dark hair pinned back, up off her neck, but thick curls still dangle, framing her face like a lion's mane. The dancer's skin is brown, her eyes are closed, her crimson lips pulled into a smile, and a single red rose lays tucked behind one ear.

"She reminds me of you," Dani says.

It's meant as a compliment, but it's hard to take that way when this music-box dancer's been abandoned to gather dust for God knows how many years. When she's something you could live without.

So in a way, I guess, she *is* like me.

"What's this?" I point to a drawer at the base of the music box, only Dani's busy winding the key, and the melody is as Latin as the dancer: a tinny re-creation of Jobim's haunting "Favela," his ode to Rio's neglected neighborhoods and their inhabitants, to the people forgotten by a nation determined not to face its own demons.

Its own failings.

The music plays and plays while the dancer spins, and I reach to open the drawer myself. Only I pull too hard, and the whole thing flies into my hands. Startled, I stare down at the drawer's contents in confusion. The music box came from a bin on one of the unclaimed shelves, meaning its owner is unknown. Yet if anyone had bothered to look inside, they would've seen what I'm seeing now—a whole stack of letters, thick ones, sealed into envelopes that have been neatly tied together with a cream-colored ribbon. There's also a message scrawled across the top envelope, handwritten in black ink. It says simply:

Read me.

"Who wrote that?" Dani whispers. "Who's it from?"

"I don't know," I say, but I intend to find out, and she does, too, I guess. Together, we settle on the floor, legs crossed, dust billowing up around us, and after setting the music box aside, Dani leans in as I pull the ribbon free. With trembling hands, I reach for the top envelope and flip it over. I'm eager to open it. Eager to know what we've found.

Or more accurately, *who* we've found.

Who it is who's no longer lost.

Not in the way that we are.

PART I:

BEFORE WE WERE MISSING

ONE

DANI

I'M PRETTY SURE that what my parents hate most about my boyfriend is the fact that he's white. That's not to say they don't like white folks. They like some of them just fine. But not for me.

"It's nothing against Roger personally," my mother said when we first started seeing each other. This was all the way back in ninth grade, almost a full two years ago, and I've heard a million variations of the same speech ever since. "But being with him gives the impression that there aren't any Black boys for you to date. It sends a message, and it's one that doesn't reflect well on our community."

Yeah, well, leave it to Emmeline Rosemarie Washington to care more about *our community* than she cares about her only daughter's happiness. But that's par for the course around here, as is my insistence on ignoring her concerns. My mother only cares about the Black community so much as it can make her look good and boost her political clout in the Dallas-Fort Worth region.

Unfortunately for Roger, he thinks she doesn't like him for other reasons. Most notably the fact that he's currently in treatment for an eating disorder that he got while trying to make weight for the wrestling team this past year. He's really good at wrestling—he made all-state and everything—but he ended up in the hospital for a month after having a seizure in front of his whole family at Christmas dinner. Super dramatic, right? But that's Roger for you. Anyway, it turned out he'd started puking his food in order to lose a few pounds; then it turned out he didn't know how to stop doing it. He still kind of doesn't, but it's not the reason my mom doesn't like him. I can't tell him this, though, because the truth isn't any better. Plus, my dad's clueless; he's always griping about stuff like eating disorders and depression being these frivolous "white people problems," ranking right up there with complaints about yachting season, fantasy football, and the constant urge to point out other people's racism without addressing one's own.

Anyway, on the days Roger doesn't have therapy, we usually go to his house after school. This is because his parents are never home and mine almost always are. Most of the time—like today—we'll fool around for a while, up in his room, but we haven't done *everything* yet. I would, I think. I mean I want to, but it's not, like, a top priority, and besides, Roger says he's not ready. Sometimes I wonder if he's into guys more than me, but most of the time I don't care.

Food, sex, you could probably say commitment's not really his thing.

"You still down for that party later? At Benny's?" I ask because it's Friday and it's getting late, and at the moment, we're just lying around on Roger's bed, eating pizza. My top's off but his isn't, and I'm actually *really* high, only Roger doesn't know this. He hates pot with the passion most people reserve for TSA pat-downs and drivers who don't pull into the intersection while making a left-hand turn. Although it's not just pot for me today, but also Xanax and Adderall and a Vicodin I stole earlier from his parents' medicine cabinet. The weed's the best of it, though. Over winter break, my cousin Abe—he's studying film at USC and thinks he's going to be the next Ryan Coogler—brought back edibles from California that come in the form of chocolate-covered blueberries, and they're kind of amazing. Popping a couple when I'm stressed makes my brain feel all marshmallow soft. Like there are no sharp edges in the world. Not anywhere.

"Sure," Roger says, meaning the party, but I can tell his heart's not in it. I can tell other things, too—like the way he runs his fingers through his hair and how he holds tension in his jaw. These are telltale signs of his anxiety. He'll still go, though, because it's what I want to do, and that's part of our bond. Looking out for one another. After all, I never told anyone about what Roger was doing to make weight last year and I still don't tell, and he's grateful for this. Just like I'm grateful he's never told anyone any of *my* secrets. We take each other at face value—for better and mostly for worse. But that's what a real relationship is, I think.

It's what makes us good together.

I pop a couple more blueberries on the drive home, but it's sort of a waste. I'll be forced to face my parents either way when I get there. Sober or not, the interaction will be intolerable.

It always is.

I make the most of the present by rolling my window down and cranking my music up. My car's cute, a little cherry-red BMW 3 Series that I got for my sixteenth birthday (I know, I know). It would be hard *not* to have fun driving this thing, although, believe me, it came with plenty of strings attached to its sexy straight-six engine. Still, I love this time of year. April in Texas means the heat hasn't turned on us yet. It's just the tornadoes you have to watch out for, but tonight the heavens above are clear.

Clear.

Clear.

My skin comes alive, and I press down on the gas. The

car lunges forward with a snarl as the wind catches my hair, my heart, and I drum my fingers against the steering wheel while Kendrick Lamar croons about sinning and not losing his vibe.

This is *everything*.

Dusk settles in as the landscape shifts from quaint suburban sameness into something more imposing. Roger and I both hail from Preston Hollow, one of the most desired enclaves in all of Dallas. However, my family lives in the Northgate neighborhood, which might just be the most desirous of all.

That probably sounds odd, considering our Blackness and the fact that Preston Hollow was purposely engineered to preserve whiteness, save any slaves or servants. But through fire and grit, my family's forged its own history here, one that started when my maternal great-grandfather, Buddy Sperling III, paid a white man to pose as the buyer so that he could purchase a not-so-modest tree-lined estate. Long story short, he and his family endured years of death threats, harassment, and worse. But not once did they consider moving.

Not once did they back down.

Up ahead, my family's Northgate home comes into view. Through the windshield, I spy its looming silhouette and feel a wave of dizziness at its size. Its showiness. The front gate's open, however, which is an unwelcome surprise. Some kind of event must be going on. Driving closer, I see dozens of cars wedged in the lower circle, far below the main house, and a valet's waiting at the base of the hill. He jogs over and gives a quick nod as I pull up.

"Good evening, miss," he says.

"Call me Dani," I tell him the way I always do.

Instead, he holds my door, and once I'm out, slides behind the wheel.

"What's going on tonight?" I ask. "Who's here?"

The valet shrugs. "Rich people."

Yeah, well, that's my guess, too. The valet drives off with my car, and with all other options gone, I start up the steep brick walkway, sweeping beneath twin birch trees and inhaling the scent of star jasmine and honeysuckle. The party appears to be isolated to the side garden, which is where my parents do most of their entertaining. Live music's a hallmark of all their events, and tonight features a live jazz band.

Peeking between rows of hedges, I spy swirls of satin and taffeta; disembodied dresses and custom suits hold cocktail glasses and plates of catered food. My head throbs with the early throes of a migraine. This has to be a charity fundraiser of some sort. Pretty much everything my parents host is a fundraiser, although can an act be considered charitable if it's done in self-interest?

Can a gift ever take more than it offers?

These are the questions that haunt me.

The last thought I have before placing my hand on the door-knob and pushing my way inside is *I wish to God I'd taken more than one Vicodin.*

Once inside, I long to be anywhere else. My breath quickens and my heart rattles as I creep through the foyer, across the living room, and head for the staircase. I'm eager to avoid detection.

Interrogation.

Whatever the hell we're calling it these days.

It's hard to pinpoint when my discontent with my family began. Growing up, I was my mother's daughter—smug, bold, and believing wholeheartedly in her vision of Black excellence. How could I not? I was a *Washington*.

To the manor born.

As a child, my life revolved around Black cotillion and Black society and Black choir. I excelled at these because I excelled at whatever I put my heart into, and whatever I put my heart into was whatever would make my mom proud. This symbiotic system worked for a while, until she craved more. I was in fourth grade when her political career took off. It started when she was elected to the local school board. Then came her tenure as the city's chief financial officer, and now she's finishing up her first term on the Dallas city council and is already planning her reelection bid.

At first, I was thrilled to see her success. It wasn't until late middle school that things began to shift. That I began to see my mother for the hypocrite she was. It started when she began voicing support for charter schools, which was a topic that had come up in my social studies class. How they were different than private schools because they were publicly funded and operated by taking money meant for all and giving it to a select few.

Well, guess who took offense to being questioned on her morals? My mother's response was to tell me I didn't know what the hell I was talking about and that education in a place like DFW was "too complex" for me to understand. Challenge accepted. I spent the next two months working feverishly on my eighth-grade social action project that highlighted the faulty logic in the charter school model, its reinforcement of racial segregation, as well as the damage done by a lack of regulation and oversight.

My project was a hit, earning me accolades and an invitation to join the honor society at my high school as an incoming freshman. I was even invited to present at a statewide education and equity conference by the time my mother figured out how to shut me down. I'd forged her signature on the conference permission paperwork and was forced to withdraw. Whatever. The damage was already done, and the tension I'd stirred up in our household was exhilarating. Shots had been fired, battle lines drawn, and ever since, I've made sure to live up to my personal motto of always knowing what the hell I'm talking about.

Oh, and also: *Cross me at your goddamn peril.*

I'm suddenly bold. Or maybe it's the blueberries. Either way, I veer off course, away from the staircase, and head for the garden. It's packed, well lit, but I elbow my way through the throng of guests and walk straight to the bar. Here, I order a gin and tonic, which I'm quickly handed, and it's a pretty drink, too—chiseled glass topped with a sprig of mint and a wedge of lime.

I drop a five in the tip jar. My heart continues its adrenaline surge, but on my return trip across the patio, I reach and snag a glass of champagne from a server's tray for good measure. Double-fisting the drinks, I cut through the kitchen and hurry up to my room. I make it, somehow, gently depositing the glasses onto my desk. My lips twitch into a smile; victory is mine.

Victory is all that matters.

Victory, however, is also short-lived; a quick glance at the clock tells me it's almost eight. *Shit.* I'm not sure how this happened, but it lights a fire under my ass to get ready. I look around for what I'll need for the party, which is more complicated than the usual "something hot," although that's important, too. But Benny Valerde doesn't live in Preston Hollow. He's from downtown by way of Jalisco, and his parties are legendary.

Tonight's is being held in the basement of an art gallery, and the theme is *Far from Heaven*. My planned outfit includes thigh-high leather boots and a riding crop, but honestly, it's kind of a cop-out. *Far from Heaven* isn't about sin, although it's fun to pretend it is. In reality, it's an old depressing movie about racism and homophobia, all centered on some tragic white lady's suburban life story and her dawning realization that she totally knows nothing about anything.

I slide my jeans off and reach for the gin and tonic. It's perfect for a sweaty spring night. Bubbles fizz up my nose and down my throat, and when I've drained the glass, I get back to work, pulling on my stockings and boots before shimmying into a tight black skirt and an even-tighter tank top. Then I reach for the champagne flute and hold it while I pose in front of the full-length mirror and admire my legs, my butt. Everything. I slap the crop against leather and smile. Roger is going to *hate* this, but I look good. Damn good.

Just like how I feel.

The Molly I've been saving in my desk drawer slides easily into the zippered pocket of my skirt. That little white pop of joy. My phone fits, too, no purse needed, and besides, it makes me cringe to see girls wearing those tiny backpacks when they go out dancing. It always looks like they've got on a turtle's shell, and I mean, that's a pretty generous interpretation.

The champagne and gin have gone to my head, a frothy rush, and I put on NCT 127's "Heartbreaker" to dance to while I vape by the window. I text Roger that I'll be coming over to get him in, like, a few minutes, and I mean to leave, I really do, but also I want more champagne, so I sneak back downstairs and get another drink and then another after that, and at some point, in one of my trips to the garden, I get cornered by this older white dude who proceeds to tell me all about his job, which is super boring and involves traveling around the world and helping large corporations do damage control after they've screwed up.

"Like *Scandal*?" I say, arching my eyebrow at him in a way I know looks devious.

"Like Union Carbide," he replies flatly.

I laugh and he doesn't, and I drink more and then I slip the Molly from my pocket and swallow it, and maybe I should be worried that Roger hasn't texted back to ask where I am, but I'm not. In fact, I'm feeling pretty fine right where I am, getting wasted in the garden of my parents' home when they haven't even noticed I'm here.

So maybe I'm not really.

Here.

The ecstasy hits, smooth and sudden, and now I'm feeling really good. So good that I pull my vape pen out and light up right there in front of everybody. Soon the man touches my shoulder and tells me I'm very pretty for my age, which is disgusting. I want to tell him I'm sixteen and that my daddy's paying for his drinks. But then I catch a glimpse of my mother. She glides by, the belle, the black swan, and I turn away, which is weird when I so desperately want to be seen. I'm feeling amazing, though, like my heart is made of clouds, real puffy ones, so once she's gone, I play coy and vape more; then I lift my phone to take a selfie while standing beneath the bobbling strands of lights and in front of the glittering surface of our pool, and even though I don't have my riding crop with me, I post the photo with the caption #FarFromHeaven and wait for Roger to like it.

He doesn't, and I wait and wait, and the more I stare at the photo of myself, the more it starts to looks as if I'm sinking below the surface of the water, not rising above it. And the more I think about *this*, the more I'm able to imagine nothing in my life is as it seems and that maybe, just maybe, all along, I've been the one starring in a depressing film about racism and homophobia, only this time it's centered on some tragic rich Black girl's suburban life story and her dawning realization that she totally knows nothing about anything.

TWO

CAMILA

FINALLY.

The end-of-day bell rings. Well, it's not a bell so much as a mindless tone emitted through the halls of Lamont-Belvedere High School at a precise decibel and register so bland, it was no doubt developed in a lab paid to produce the sound most likely to compel obedience and subdue our violent impulses. Regardless, the response is Pavlovian; in an instant, the classroom awakens, transforming into a blur of movement as students gather their bags, their belongings, and head for the door.

I stand to follow suit. Joining the herd goes against my better instincts, but what choice do I have? Only before I can make my escape, Mr. Hutchinson calls my name and asks me to stay.

In response, a couple of boys sneer and make sex sounds at me, these high-pitched porny moans, but I nod dutifully and walk over to his desk. I actually like Mr. Hutchinson, and I even kind of like precalc, but at the moment, I don't have it in me to be peppered with questions like *Is something wrong?* and *How can I help?* and *I've noticed a change, Camila. I'm worried.* Okay, this last one isn't a question, but hearing it makes me feel so *guilty.* Like I'm a terrible person. And what I want to say in return is *Please stop caring* and *I'm not worth bothering about,* but instead I go with:

"I can't stay late today. I have dance at three."

"Of course." Mr. Hutchinson sighs and gestures toward the plate-glass window, the one overlooking the surrounding prairie grass that's already turning brown in the heat. "Well, then let's check in another time. You be safe out there."

"Sure thing." I grab my stuff and flee. It's a nice sentiment, but like his concern about my grades, Mr. Hutchinson's warning can't do anything to protect me. What's "out there" at the moment is the noxious and unrelenting stench of raw sewage that's settled over the town of Lamont, Georgia, of late. During the school day, the windows are sealed shut, and the air is set to recirculate. But the smell's still there. It's always there. A foulness that clings to our clothes, seeps into our skin, and haunts our dreams.

This unpleasantness is due to twists of both fate and topography. Lamont has the misfortune to sit at sea level in an open valley bordered on all sides by craggy foothills. Air flow isn't exactly a gift from the gods around here, meaning there's no place for the stench to go. The more relevant fact, however, is that we're located sixty miles north of Bucksville, Georgia, which is an even smaller and more rural town that's home to a private waste dump site that makes a profit shipping in human waste from New York on railroad cars. Unfortunately, the site's owners happen to be snarled in a legal battle with Bucksville, a conflict that has temporarily halted operations and left their most recent inbound train stranded in its literal tracks—right here in Lamont.

To put it mildly, the heat wave showing up last week really amplified the issue. Not to mention it provided rich fodder for late-night jokes and a hell of a lot of Twitter roasting, seeing as we're not the first Southern town to get a Northern "poop train" stuck within its city limits. But you want to know the worst thing about it all? Beyond the humiliating jokes and memes and the wretched smell that's sickened our residents and led to the cancellation of pretty much every outdoor event planned this spring, Bucksville's sweltering poop train has also delivered an existential crisis to our city's doorstep. Because with every breath we take, over and over, the citizens of Lamont are reminded that when it comes to corporate profit and greed, the dignity and humanity of more than five thousand people is worth far less than shit.

Before stepping outside, I pull my breathing mask on over my mouth and nose. It's one of the heavy-grade industrial ones, the kind they've been handing out to students so that we keep coming to school. Technically the masks are meant to protect us from smoke, air pollution, and global pandemics, but they also help with the smell. In theory, at least.

Ninety-degree heat, and I have to run through the streets of Lamont at top speed. But being late isn't an option. Not today. This moment is one I've planned for meticulously over the past few months. Maybe my whole lifetime. It's my last and best shot out of here.

For good.

The dance studio looms ahead. Brushing sweat from my forehead, I slow to a walk and gird myself for crossing the parking lot that teems with SUVs and duelies, all bumping and jockeying for a precious spot despite ample street parking. It's wild, but it's also the best metaphor for Lamont I've ever seen. This town's powered by hierarchies, like where you park or what pew you sit in at church. Even stuff like what team you root for or what flags are flying outside your house (hint: they're not all American) dictate how people treat you.

Darting around the vehicles and managing to avoid certain death, I burst into the studio, wave at Hannah at the front desk, then bolt down the hallway as I slide my mask off. The door to room 104 is half-open, and I hate myself for the timid way I poke my head in. Ask if I can enter. My voice is grating even to my own ears, but the point is that today is for me. I rented this room myself with money I earned selling fried dough at the dirt raceway last summer, and I don't need to ask permission. I need to own this space.

I need it to be mine.

Ivan's already here. He's standing in the back with the tripod and smiles at the sight of me. "You made it!"

I drop my backpack on the ground, start kicking off my shoes. "Sorry I'm late."

"Not late at all. I'm still getting the camera set up and everything. Go change. Warm up. We'll get this going as soon as you're ready. There's no rush."

"Thanks." I duck back down the hall to the changing room, which is full of little girls in pink tutus. Most of them are blond and indistinguishable from one another, but their energy is infectious, the way they bounce off one another and bubble with laughter at the tiniest things. I'm not studying ballet right now, but I did when I was younger, and I still remember how uncomfortable I felt back then. I'd fixate endlessly on my curly hair and dark sun-kissed skin, the way I stood out in a room full of Georgia whiteness. It's one of the reasons I switched to contemporary, but even when I complained about ballet standards, my mama would just try and convince me that the reason I stood out is because I was the prettiest. But it never felt that way to me, and besides, no one but her was saying it. My beauty—if I had any—had yet to find its beholder.

After grabbing clothes from my locker, I change in one of the bathroom stalls—pulling on my tights, skirt, and leotard in private so that no one sees anything I don't want them to. This includes the scars and the bruising but also a shuddering cloudburst of tears that threatens to overwhelm me until I ball my fists and bite my cheek and pound my ribs into submission.

Pain is stronger than sorrow, they say. It's also weakness leaving the body and the path to wisdom and fuel for the journey, and, no, it's not good to hurt myself, not at all, but it also makes me who I am.

Pain, that is.

My own.

When I'm ready, I adjust my top, leave the stall, and stand before the mirror to do my hair—twisting it into a tight knot and using coconut oil to tame the edges. Next come the pins and the hairnet and a heck of a lot of hairspray. Lastly, I blot my lips with a hint of stain, refresh my eyeliner, and that's it. I'm done. The ballet girls have all gathered to watch, and they stare up at me, lured in by the air of authority I project. It's not authority I *feel*, but I'll be damned if I'm going to let them see me as anything but confident.

I take a step back. Smooth my skirt.

"What're you dancing?" one of the little girls asks before I leave.

"Modern," I say.

"For a show?"

"For my life," I tell her.

Back in room 104, Ivan's got the camera ready and the lighting's all set up. He's also cued my music, and I melt a little at how thoughtful he's being but quickly shove that thought away. Gratitude has no role in success. It leads to obligation, which leads to distraction, which is how I won't let myself fail. Not again.

Besides, Ivan's the studio owner's son—only two years older than I am—meaning he's got a financial incentive to help me. I'm not fool enough to fall for temptation like that, but even my thinking about it probably tells you something about the depths of my loneliness—that my mind so willingly conjures up some imaginary kinship between the two of us. It's pathetic, really, and it's why I'm getting out of this place. Towns like Lamont crush girls who don't leave, fooling them into believing that squeezing out some asshole's brat is part of God's plan. And then what? You get to spend a lifetime wondering what might've been? No way.

"You ready?" Ivan asks once I've warmed up, once I've gone through my cues and marked the room.

"As I'll ever be," I reply.

"You tell your parents yet?"

"No," I snap, and it's shitty, I know. But my parents have enough to deal with at the moment—especially my dad, who's in public works. The damn poop train's giving him an ulcer these days, and anyway, if I get in this time, then we can talk. But for now, the anxiety, the stress, the sleeplessness—that's for me to deal with. No one else. "Come on. Let's go."

Ivan crouches in front of the viewfinder. "Remember, we can always do more than one take."

"No way."

He looks up. "Why not?"

"If I were auditioning live, I'd only get one chance."

"But you're not doing it live. So it doesn't matter."

"It matters to me," I say sternly. "I want to do this right."

Ivan shrugs. "You're going to nail it anyway."

"I haven't yet."

"You *will*. Cams, you've improved so much this year. I know you don't see it, but that school would be foolish not to take you."

"I'll be foolish if I don't give them a reason to." And with that, I step up to my mark and push my shoulders back. I start this piece in second position, with my hips and feet rotated outward. My arms are pulled in tight to my core, tense, waiting.

Ivan shoots me a thumbs-up. Then presses play on the audio.

It starts.

The music.

My body explodes. A kinesthetic unfurling of limbs that flings me over wooden floorboards and sends me spinning through space. I land, leap again, and again after that, and while perfection is something I'll always be chasing, always be striving for, I'm also wholly aware of the beauty I'm creating and the emotions my performance will evoke. It'll be passion and flame; exhilaration and bold-faced wonder.

Yet all I feel is empty.

Later that night, I sit in front of the laptop I've coerced Ivan into loaning me, writing and rewriting my letter to the admissions team at the Fieldbrook Academy of Performing Arts in Pompton Lakes, New Jersey. It's a struggle to put words to how much I want this. Like the limited roads out of Lamont, there aren't a lot of entry points into a professional dance career, which is the only thing I've ever wanted out of life. The only dream I've ever chased.

But it never pays to be desperate. Finally, I settle on:

Dear Admissions Committee members,

Thank you for your kind invitation to once again submit my application for your consideration, and thank you also for waiving the application fee. I took your advice from last year to heart and have been working diligently on my technique and artistic expression. This should be evident in my most recent audition, which I have uploaded to your account via Slideroom. As I think you know, attending Fieldbrook and studying with your amazing faculty has been a dream of mine for years, and I very much hope to hear from you soon.

Sincerely,

Camila M. Ortiz

My finger hovers over the send button. I feel sweaty, sick. Definitely unworthy. I don't think I can do this. I don't think I deserve to.

But third time's a charm, I tell myself.

This time I have to make it.

This time I have to be what they want.

Right?

THREE

DANI

YEAH, WELL, APPARENTLY, getting trashed at your parents' charity event for local at-risk youth and having photos of you drinking, dancing, and later passing out make their way online and into the local media with headlines such as "Irony Alert" or "What Tree Did This Apple Fall From?" is one approach to getting your parents' full attention. Too bad I never wanted any of it in the first place.

"What were you *thinking*?" my father bellows the next morning, all while waving his iPad around in my face to show me the scandal, the photos. Oh, the horror. Okay, it *is* pretty bad, but he's so angry, spit's flying out of his mouth like a dragon, which is kind of funny, and also it turns out I've woken up in a downstairs guest bedroom, which I absolutely don't remember coming into *at all*. Unfortunately, it would appear that while I was sleeping it off, my parents went through my room, through everything, and, well, it's all out on the table now. Like, literally. It's actually spread out on the nightstand table. The Adderall. The Xanax. The Oxy.

Some other things, too.

Did I mention this was bad?

With my stomach lurching and my memory hazy, I sit up to face my father's rage, and the thing is, I *want* to say something. Fight for my truth. But I can't find the words. Not the right ones, at least, and I wonder if this is what Roger felt like when he woke up from his seizure on the floor of his parents' bathroom to find them staring back at him.

Like he knew the game was up.

"I wasn't," I'm able to say at last, and my mouth feels dry, parched.

"What?" he barks.

"I wasn't thinking," I tell him. "That was the last thing I was doing."

"Then what were you doing?" My head swivels. This question comes from my mom, who's standing on the other side of the room. Compared to my dad's eye-popping rage and iPad-waving histrionics, she seems almost calm. Measured.

This *terrifies* me.

"I was . . . I was just trying to feel good. I was supposed to be going out with Roger, but I drank too much. It was irresponsible. I know that."

"You know I spoke with Roger this morning, and he informed me that this wasn't your first time mixing substances or blowing him off. He says you've been getting high a lot this year. Or, as he puts it, 'self-medicating.'"

"*Roger* said that?"

My mother settles on the bed beside me. She's beautiful, as always, soft locs falling shoulder length to frame her high cheekbones and perfect skin, and I mean, would it kill her to get a zit every now and then? "He also says that he thinks you're unhappy. Is that right?"

I fume. "Roger's not right about anything. You trust a white boy to tell you how I feel?"

"Oh, he's just some white boy now?" she chides. "Not the person you spend all your time with? The one you told me was your soul mate?"

Jesus. Did I really say that? "He doesn't know me at all."

"I have a hard time believing that," my mother says.

"You don't know me any better than he does."

"Not if you won't let me."

"You're pathetic." I flash. "You're just pretending to care about me because I made you look bad."

"I care because you're my *daughter*," she says.

"Yeah, well, that wasn't my choice."

"None of us have a choice about that."

"Oh, please," I snap. "Grown women have choices. It's the *law*."

My mother snorts. "In Texas?"

I stare at her. "Are you saying you didn't want me?"

"I didn't say that at all."

"You're such a coward," I hiss. "You wouldn't tell me if it were the truth."

"Dani," my father warns, but my mother holds a hand up.

"Deflecting's not going to work this time, sweetie." She edges closer, and the thing is, she's still so infuriatingly *calm*. "You think I don't know what you're doing? Trying to change the subject by aiming all your failures back onto me? You're not my daughter for nothing, you know. I practically invented that trick."

I say nothing. I have a bad feeling about this. Really bad. So I glance at my father, who won't meet my eye. "Daddy, what's she talking about?"

"Listen to your mother," he says.

"But why aren't you saying anything?"

"You don't want to hear what I have to say right now."

"Oh, go on, Warren," my mother urges. "This has to come from both of us. I can't be the bad guy here."

"Okay, fine." My father scowls. "We've tried hard to raise you with the right values. With the right sense of morals and decency. And this is what you do? This is how you repay us?"

"I already said I was sorry."

"My idea was to take away all your privileges for a few months. No car. No phone. No internet. No spring break. Nothing. But your mom came up with a different idea, and I happen to think she's on target with it. There's no negotiating on this, either, Dani. You're going."

I freeze. "Going where?"

My mother reaches to put a hand on my mine. "Sweetie, addiction isn't something you can deal with just by willpower."

"I'm not *addicted*—"

Her hand squeezes. "We want you to get help, and there's nothing wrong with needing help."

"But I don't need it!"

"There are so many households in the country who are dealing with similar problems. It's not anything to be ashamed of. Just think how much good we can do by setting an example and taking this issue seriously. Transparency is everything. It helps break down stigma. Encourages others to get help. Don't you think that's important?"

"What're you talking about?"

"We've talked to some members of the community, and based on what they've recommended, we've decided that it would be best for you to enter treatment at a recovery clinic out in Tucson. It's called Horizon Home, and they specialize in addiction. You'll get straightened out, and it'll be no big deal. Everyone will see that we Washingtons face our struggles head-on." A glow radiates from my mother as she speaks, and I realize, in some small way, she's enjoying this. Crafting the narrative the way she crafts her campaign speeches.

"*Our* struggles?" I echo.

She lifts her chin. "You think this doesn't reflect on me? That I don't wonder what I could've done differently?"

"This is about you now?"

"I never said that."

"Well, I'm not going to Tucson just to make you look good. I'm not going anywhere, because there's nothing wrong with me. I'm not an addict!"

"I'm afraid you don't have a choice in the matter," my mother says.

My jaw tightens. "Fucking Texas, right?"

"Your flight's on Monday morning. We'll fly out with you. Make sure you get settled."

"And then, what, you'll do an interview with the local news? Put out a press release?"

I'm into it now, ready to fight, but for once, my parents don't respond. Instead, in what is clearly a preplanned attack, my father drops a brochure for this Horizon Home place on my lap—the words "faith-based approach" jump out at me—and then they leave. Although not before scooping up all the drugs and paraphernalia and taking it with them so my junkie ass can't do something crazy like swallow it all or put it in a glass pipe and smoke it.

I would, you know. Just to spite them.

Once they're gone, I scramble from bed, moaning a little at my hangover, and well, the good news is that I find my blueberry edibles buried beneath the blankets because, apparently, I brought them to bed with me last night. Good job, past Dani.

After rage-eating a couple and shooting an angry text to Roger (*It's over, dickhead. You'd better watch your back*), I set out to do what I should've done years ago, when I first realized how toxic my life was and how it was all centered here, in this house, in the hearts of my own parents.

I start planning my escape.

FOUR

CAMILA

I AWAKE IN A SWEAT. My brain knows where I am—in bed, in my own room. But that's not the problem. Sitting up in total darkness, I kick off the blankets, then claw at my throat. God, it's so *hot*. Heat you can choke on.

Reaching for the glass on my nightstand, I pull it close and chug down. The water's tepid, tasteless, but soothes my parched throat. Years of dance have schooled me well in the art of hydration, and I can picture my organs literally sopping up molecules out of my bloodstream to replace what's been lost to this sweltering heat wave.

Flipping onto my hands and knees, I crawl forward and peer through the cracked window my headboard juts up against. The streetlamps are off, and the only thing visible is an angled slice of driveway. The rest of the world lies thick with shadow, and I have the urge to join the darkness, the solitude. The sheer absence of life.

Instead I do the one thing I shouldn't, which is to grab my phone from under my pillow and check my email. It's been nine days since I sent in my Fieldbrook audition, and other than a cursory "Thank you. We've received your submission and look forward to reviewing it" auto-reply, there's been no response. Last year, it took them twelve days to reject me. The year before, thirteen. I guess I have it in my mind that different is good and sooner is better, so not checking is pretty much impossible.

Only, there's no email.

There's nothing.

A wave of self-loathing washes over me, and I lurch forward to bang my skull against the headboard. Then I bang it again for good measure and promise not to check my phone for another twelve hours. If I can't be disciplined, then I don't deserve to get in.

I slide off the bed and slip on a T-shirt. It's too early to be up, but I refuse to chase sleep I know my brain won't grant me, and so I turn to more immediate needs; my bladder's full and also my left ring finger's throbbing with this low-grade tenderness. Always a nail biter, I tore the cuticle a few days back, and now it feels as if some sort of infection's taken hold.

It's an odd sensation—traversing the bare wood hallway as

my parents lie in slumber above. For the past eight months, they've devoted every spare minute to converting our home's unfinished attic into the master suite of their dreams. A tedious project if there ever was one, but last month, the project was finally complete. Giddy at their accomplishment, they promptly emptied out the bedroom next to mine and moved upstairs.

In truth, I was as eager as they were for the attic's completion. Running the length of the house, their new space is expansive, open, punctuated by slanted ceilings and windows facing every direction. My father, who grew up with nothing and eternally craves beauty, now has an unfettered view of the wildflowers behind our home. They're the ones he loves to paint, and when my mother's not caring for her decidedly un-wild garden, she's fond of venturing into the meadow, snipping a few blooms, and dunking them into pitchers and vases as offerings of inspiration.

So I get why my parents wanted a place of their own. I wanted them to have it, too. But their absence still stings on mornings like this. It's the knowledge that they've purposely ascended somewhere I can't reach.

Somewhere I was never meant to go.

After locking the bathroom door, I switch on the light and fan. Then I run hot water in the sink while I sit to pee and count the cracks in the checkered subway tile running beneath my bare feet. By the time I'm done, a cloud of steam has started to fill the room. I hop up and thrust my sore finger beneath the faucet flow.

The water *scalds*. My instinct's to pull back, but it's not through sacrifice one finds salvation. It's through suffering. Always the suffering. The wiry pink-and-gray scars running along the inside of my thighs and under my arms are proof of this. Although today's not a day I reach for the razor blade I keep tucked behind the base of the toilet. I've vowed not to do it again until I hear back from Fieldbrook. In this case, waiting's the real suffering, and as such, the only path toward grace.

Back in my room, I stand naked on the carpet while I brush my hair. It's long, dark, and used to be lustrous. Now strands of it are floating to the ground. Gently, though, and lit by morning light. A few more strokes and then I can't help myself. I pick up my phone once again and check.

Christ, you're so goddamn weak

My heart stutters.

You deserve nothing

There's an email.

You talentless bitch

With a subject line that reads *Congratulations* . . .

My hands are shaking and I'm on the verge of puking by the time I hear my parents shuffling around upstairs. But this means my tactics have worked: I started breakfast ten minutes ago in an attempt to lure them to me with the smell of sizzling bacon. Hot coffee. English muffins in the toaster.

My dad's first to arrive. He walks into our small dining nook, and I know this is a performance I've got to nail. I press my lips into a smile and shove his favorite mug into his hands. I'm a little too enthusiastic, but he manages. No coffee spills.

"Thanks," he says as I take in the darkness beneath his eyes, the slight tremor of his grip. I love my father, but he hasn't had an easy life, and happiness tends to elude him. Or not happiness, exactly. That's too fleeting an emotion. People feel happy when they watch professional wrestling on television or listen to our unhinged president scream about how tremendous he is. But my dad struggles to maintain any sense of well-being, which he usually perceives as indulgence.

"You okay?" I ask.

He smiles. "Just tired. I've got a lot of work these days."

I know he means the awful poop train, since he's part of the delegation tasked with negotiating with both the state and the waste management company to get it out of Lamont. "Is Mama up yet?"

"Not yet." My dad slides his glasses on and peers at the food I'm cooking. "What's the occasion?"

"I've got some good news, Daddy. Really good news." These words feel funny on my tongue, like my mouth is reluctant to release them.

"What's that?" My dad sips his coffee.

"I got in, Daddy." I'm beaming now. I can't help it.

"In?"

Joy bubbles in my throat before spilling out. "To Fieldbrook. The dance academy. I didn't want to tell you and Mama that I'd applied again. Not after the last two years. I didn't want to disappoint you. But they invited me to audition by tape, and I got in this time! I just found out."

Water comes on in the upstairs shower, a sudden overhead downpour. I glance up instinctively. That's how new and rare this sound is.

"I can go, Daddy, right?" I return to the sizzling bacon, ready to pluck it from the cast-iron pan. When there's no answer, I whirl around, tongs in hand. The look on my father's face is one of guilt and shame and also shock.

Then it hits me: the utter folly and stupidity of hope. The utter folly and stupidity of *me*. Because I never bothered to tell my parents I was auditioning again and that I hadn't abandoned my dream of going away to school.

So now I'm not.

FIVE

DANI

I LEAVE THAT NIGHT. After nursing my hangover (totally genuine) and hiding in my room all day, I bide my time and wait until my parents are in bed. They're nothing if not predictable, and once I'm sure they're asleep, I down an Adderall and also half a Provigil because those have been making the rounds at school lately. Nootropics don't have anything on real amphetamines, but they help to clear my mind.

Expansively.

Brilliantly.

Soon the buzz kicks in, and my heart starts to do its drum-roll thing. This is when I know it's time. With a metaphoric spring in my step, I pull my packed suitcase (it's this Tumi hard shell I got last summer when we went to Bali, and it's the prettiest sea-blue color you've ever seen) out of my closet and stuff in the last few items that I'm going to need: my passport, vape pen, and, most importantly, the envelope filled with cash that I've been saving in my desk drawer for the past year, if not more.

Most of it's birthday money, but there's a chunk I earned last year doing event planning for my dad. He's so clueless. It's not like he hired me through any official process, either. What happened is that he needed help organizing this faculty retreat for his department heads. But because he didn't vet vendors in time to get through the contracted bidding process, he just paid me cash under the table to do it. In the end, all I did was make some spreadsheets and figure out the schedule and print some name tags. But that kind of stuff is beyond him.

Once I reach the first floor, I duck into my mother's office. There's one last thing I need to do, and it requires access to her phone. Sure enough, it's plugged in and resting on her desk, all snug in the little monogrammed oxblood leather case that she bought for the damn thing. I seriously can't imagine why anyone would want to latch and unlatch a leather case each time they check their phone, but that's my mom for you. She'll choose image over substance.

Every.

Goddamn.

Time.

After undoing the latch, I quickly type in her password—the one she thinks I don't know but I always have. It's *sperlingbabe*, by the way, which, barf. From the main screen, I scroll through her settings, and I'm no hacker or anything. I mean, I'm not even particularly technologically inclined, but both my parents have pretty much zero common sense when it comes to privacy protection.

That's probably what she thinks the leather case is for, now that I think about it. I was the one who had to change the passwords on all the smart appliances they bought so that the internet won't spy on us. Although I talked them out of installing a doorbell cam, thank God. I compared it to people sending their DNA off to private companies. Why on earth would anyone *pay* to make what's private public? Your home, your genetic code—hold that shit close. Anyway, the point is that it takes me all of twenty seconds to delete my phone line from the main family group, effectively rendering her unable to track me via the Find My Phone app or any other GPS monitoring system.

When I'm done, I put her phone back, grab my suitcase, and go.

SIX

CAMILA

I SING A SONG of the saints of God . . .

Clinging to shadows, I hurry along the asphalt, desperate not to be seen. I'm also cold. It's late, after midnight, and the wind blowing down Main Street's got a real bite to it.

I grit my teeth and pull my fleece close. Even with the night chill, I don't mind being outside. I crave it, actually, after being cooped up for so long. You see, the good news around here is that the poop train left town yesterday, taking with it the awful stench that had come to permeate our lives.

Inhaling cool fresh air sans mask feels wrong, but it's also right, and I know my dad must be overjoyed—or at least relieved to be untethered from this burden he never asked for. But it's not like he'd ever say that. His outlook doesn't allow joy. He's always planning for the next disaster. And anyway, ever since our conversation yesterday morning, the only emotion I've felt wafting off him is guilt. Hot, horrible guilt.

My chest squeezes, and I walk faster, slipping in my earbuds and cranking the music on my phone I've chosen for just this occasion—my favorite Cali salsa, the one with the fiery offbeat and a driving sense of urgency. My body comes alive with the shots and shimmers of the timbales, and the music rolls through me to grip my hips. My heart.

My everything.

When the tears come, they come fast, stinging and spilling down my cheeks as I break into a run. The pills I've brought rattle and shake from my jacket pocket, a soothing offbeat reminder of the end they'll bring. An end already foretold with nothing to look forward to. No hope for escape.

It won't be long, I tell myself.

This'll be over soon.

The streets are empty this late at night, and up ahead is what I've come for—the Fourth Street Bridge. Let me tell you, it's the prettiest stage in all of Lamont, lit up by hundreds of globes of golden light and stretched across the swirling depths of the Lamont River. I've always loved coming here, but especially at night, where it feels as if the whole damn universe can see you. That's what I'm here for, to touch the sky and stars and even beyond, because when I'm done, I plan on crawling down to the shoreline and ending this misery. Saying my goodbyes.

But first—

My last dance.

SEVEN

DANI

"LET ME IN!" I'm pounding the door as hard as I can. I don't know what else to try. The doorbell didn't get me any results, but I *know* someone's in there.

"Aunt Bea!" I call out. "It's me, Dani. I told you I was coming!" Okay, actually, that last part isn't true, but I shout it anyway because there's a couple across the well-lit street walking a pair of pug dogs, and they're totally staring. Plus, I *meant* to text my aunt ahead of time, only I couldn't because I don't have my phone anymore, which is, like, a whole other story. At least I didn't lose her address. I can't express how relieved I was to find

the envelope for the birthday card she'd sent me last month floating around in the bottom of my purse.

Still no answer. I hop up and down like a child because
the worst thing about this situation is that I have to pee. See,
my car got towed somewhere in Tennessee, which really
sucked seeing as I wasn't allowed to get it out without making
a call to my parents. That kind of defeated the whole "running
away" thing, so the rest of my journey to Atlanta has been via
public transit and hitchhiking, and my access to clean bath-
rooms has been limited for the past forty-eight hours. I'm not
even ashamed to admit that once the Adderall and Provigil ran
out, I had to resort to purchasing a little Greyhound meth in
order to stay awake. Falling asleep on the bus was not a chance I
was willing to take.

I knock again, but the peeing situation's getting desperate. I hop back down the porch steps, suitcase and purse in tow,
and stand on the sidewalk, staring up at the house. The pug
couple shuffles on, but I wait a few beats, allowing my gaze to
wander. The street my aunt lives on is quaint, tidy, full of trees.
It's a quiet neighborhood of homes, nothing showy—she left
that behind in Northgate, and that's what's brought me here, I
suppose.

When no one's visible, I make a dash for it, darting around
the side of the house and slipping through a wooden gate to enter

my aunt's backyard. The minute it's shut, I'm already tugging up my skirt, squatting in the shadows, near the base of the house. I'm nearly done when I hear what sounds like a door sliding open or a window sliding shut. This is followed by furtive rustling or heavy breathing of some sort.

In an instant, I'm on my feet, scrambling to get my underwear back up and my skirt back down. My bags are in my arms when a dog comes around the side of the house. A spaniel, I think. It's white with orange blotches and has medium-length silky hair. The animal trots right toward me, its quivering nose tilted up in the air.

"Go *away*." I wave frantically at the creature. Shit. My aunt Bea definitely didn't have a dog when I visited her last summer. I don't even think she *likes* dogs.

I turn to bolt as the animal lunges.

"Get off!" I snarl and kick, but it's hopeless. The dog barks once, then gets its prickly teeth wrapped around the bottom of my purse. I pull and it pulls, and I pull harder, and right then, the side yard sprinklers come on and proceed to spray us both.

The dog releases the purse with a yelp, and I fly backward, slamming to the ground with a groan. For an instant, I'm too stunned to move, but when I'm able to breathe again, I roll slowly onto my side and see that the contents of my purse have been scattered all over the place.

I start grabbing what I can before everything gets ruined by the sprinklers. The bricks are wet, mossy, and my knees keep sliding, but I'm careful to avoid the shards of glass, which represent the remains of a rum bottle I'd been hanging on to.

"Hey!" a voice says sharply. "What do you think you're doing?"

A flashlight's in my face. I throw an arm over my eyes and leap back, sprinklers thwapping at my ankles. The light lowers, revealing the man's face. He's Black, which might be a relief except for the fact that he's wearing some sort of law enforcement uniform and possibly has a gun holstered to his hip.

My legs start to shake. This is bad. Really bad.

"What are you doing?" the man repeats.

"I—I'm looking for my aunt," I fumble. "She lives here. Her name's Beatrice Miller."

"Is she expecting you? Does she know you're here?"

"I'm her *niece*."

"So if I were to ask Ms. Miller about her niece visiting, she'd say she's expecting you?"

I hesitate. If there were ever a time to come clean, to admit I'm a runaway and desperate and that I'm looking for the one family member who maybe would be willing to help me out during a crappy time when my life's falling apart, this would be it.

"Um, yeah," I tell this man in uniform. "She's definitely expecting me."

"Hey, Bea." He turns and hollers into the darkness behind him. "Someone claiming to be your niece is here. In our backyard."

My heart sinks, and just when I think it's at its absolute lowest, I hear a familiar voice call back: *"Who?"*

EIGHT

CAMILA

MY WISH REMAINS UNGRANTED.

I'm still here.

And I still don't want to be.

PART II:

WHEN WE WEREN'T LOOKING TO BE FOUND

CAMILA

TURNS OUT YOU don't get to make a lot of choices for yourself after an overdose. Especially one that's intentional and involves the police finding you and a subsequent ambulance ride to the hospital. In some logical way, this probably makes sense, but it's maddening to be told you can no longer move freely through the world. That everything you do or that is done to you will now be dictated by doctors and "best practices" and whatever the hell your shell-shocked parents have been talked into authorizing.

Anyway, I spend a couple days in the local ICU. This is a time period that involves my body being tethered to all sorts of tubes and wires, and I don't remember a lot of it. There's apparently a lot of grave concern about my heart function and other organ damage, but in the end, it's fine and eventually I'm transferred to the psych ward. Only once I'm there, I'm told I can't stay.

My singular desire is for sleep, that's all, but a doctor comes in almost immediately and asks me a lot of questions about why I did what I did and what made me feel that way, and I try and answer honestly. I tell her about getting into Fieldbrook, and how my parents no longer have the money to send me. They spent their savings on transforming our house into the space of their dreams, and I don't blame them for that, I say. If anything, *I'm* to blame for putting them in this situation and making them feel like shit, which means I'm a selfish daughter with no appreciation for what I have.

For all I've been given.

"I guess I hate myself," I tell her.

"And the cutting?" she asks, nodding at my scars. "How long has that been going on?"

"I don't know."

"How old were you when it first started?"

"Nine," I say numbly. "Maybe earlier."

"Have you ever attempted suicide before? Have you tried to end your life?"

"I'm not sure."

"How are you not sure?"

The words feel empty on my tongue. "I don't think I've

tried to die or end my life, but I also don't think I've ever really wanted to live."

"Ever?"

"Not that I can remember," I say. "Not really. But my memory, it's hard right now to think of things. To know what's true."

The doctor pats my arm. "I understand. We're trying to find a facility to transfer you to. One that specializes in adolescent psychiatric concerns."

"But why?" I ask weakly.

"To provide you with better care. This hospital is really for emergencies only. But there are places that can keep you safe and also offer real treatment and therapy for what you've been going through. Okay?"

"No," I say. "That's not what I was asking."

"What were you asking?"

"Why bother?"

TEN

DANI

BE COOL, I TELL MYSELF from the front seat of my aunt's Durango. *This is no big deal.*

This is a sentiment I believe intellectually, but my jiggling knees and knotted stomach tell a different story. The irony of this scenario does not escape me. After running away from home in order to avoid going to some drug treatment program, I've now chosen to avoid going home by entering a totally different drug treatment program.

"It's got an excellent reputation," my aunt insists more than once during our car ride, which is a mantra she's been repeating for the past three days while she's negotiated with both the facility and my parents on my behalf. Her friend's the director, apparently, and this is somewhat reassuring, even if I have no intention of actually doing anything while I'm there. I've agreed to a two-week stay—and my aunt got my parents to pay for it—but that's it. That's all they'll get from me.

"I'm glad," I tell Aunt Bea, since she's gone to so much trouble.

"I know a lot of people in the mental health field. They all say Peach Tree Hills is the best place for adolescent girls, especially girls of color. The staff is very diverse and sensitive to context and culture. You're lucky to get in, that they had a bed for you. That's not always the case. They're very selective about who they invite."

Yeah, well, I bet my parents' money is the kind of *cultural context* they're sensitive to. Like my mom says about college— there's almost always a place if you're full pay. "I thought this was just a spot to dry out. I'm not looking for a sorority bid."

Aunt Bea flicks her blinker on as she merges from one country road to the next. "They deal with a lot of different issues and have a reputation for their 'nontraditional' treatment model."

"What's that supposed to mean?"

"My understanding is that they feel the classic model of in-patient treatment is too restrictive for most young people. The lack of freedom inhibits healthy emotional development. Therefore, the aim is to provide a naturalistic environment that allows for safe exploration."

"Sounds like a zoo."

"It's not a zoo."

"Is there a breeding program?" I ask. "Teenage husbandry. I might be into that."

She sighs. "Obviously, they do a lot of screening before accepting a client, and not everybody has the same experience, but their reputation is excellent. From what I've heard, they really take a holistic and personal approach."

I sniff. "Maybe they should apply that holistic approach to their name. Reminds me of a funeral home."

My aunt doesn't respond.

"Man, it's really out in the middle of nowhere, huh?" I lean forward and peer through the windshield. We've just been driving through suburb after suburb. It's all very picturesque. Not the hordes of good ol' boys and treason flags that I expected from rural Georgia.

"We're only thirty miles from Atlanta," my aunt says. "And we're almost there."

"Hey, does it cost a lot, though?" I ask. "This fancy, nontraditional place with the good reputation? How much are my parents having to shell out?"

Aunt Bea purses her lips. "Is *that* what you're worried about?"

Sunlight breaks through the clouds, filling the car with a golden warmth as we come through a thicket of trees and over a rise. My pulse quickens as I spot a neatly lettered sign on the shoulder reading: *Peach Tree Hills Residential Care Home— 1 Mile.*

"I'm not worried about anything," I say breezily. "Nothing at all."

ELEVEN

CAMILA

PEACH TREE HILLS.

The words are chiseled into a stone sign as gray as my heart. As gray as my whole existence, such as it is. And these days, it's not much.

Idling at the facility's front gate, my dad leans out the driver's side window of his beat-up Ford, attempting to speak into the intercom and gain entrance to this place my parents have chosen to leave me. He's too far from the speaker, however, and has to put the car in park and actually get out of the vehicle, which is a nightmare to witness. It physically hurts to see how much he's fumbling this task. Technology's not his thing despite having a degree in civil engineering, and he tends to take all failure personally. Mom's too polite to say anything, which doesn't help matters any and never has.

I twist my head and gaze out the window. From the back seat, I can't see much of this place I'm being exiled to simply for the sin of trying to leave this world. Admittedly, I've also failed at a lot of things lately. I failed at killing myself. Then, after getting kicked out of the adult psych ward, my parents enrolled me in this intensive day treatment program for teens. I guess it's the kind of thing that's for when insurance doesn't want to spring for room and board. Because even though I got to sleep at home, day treatment meant I was locked in a medical center eight hours a day for two full weeks. Plus, it was all the way out in Dalton, which is known as the "Carpet Capital of the World," if you want a hint at how depressing the vibe there is.

Anyway, I failed at the day treatment, too. When it ended, I was deemed "stable," and no longer in active crisis, yet my parents were urged to find another program that would take me. Preferably residential this time and preferably "nontraditional," we were told, whatever the hell that means. Well, I guess it means a place that will harbor your kid who's no longer actively suicidal but also won't say she's sorry she tried.

On my last day in Dalton, the therapist I was working with tried bright-siding me about the future: "You know, Peach Tree

Hills is a good place. They can really help get into some of the deeper issues in your life—not just symptom management."

"How so?" I asked.

"Well, the focus there is more on your overall wellness than treating a specific diagnosis."

"You mean like a spa?"

"Not exactly," she admitted. "But I have a feeling it'll be good for you—the change of scenery and perspective. Plus, everyone is young and vibrant. You all have so much life ahead of you."

"Yeah, well, that's the problem," I'd croaked, my vocal cords still stubbornly raw and weakened by the ER efforts to revive me that I'd never consented to. That I never would consent to. Not when so many on this earth are in need of a miracle. Why give it to the one who doesn't want it?

Lost in the vista, my head swims and droops. This place might be pretty, I think, if it were Fieldbrook, and in another universe, another dimension, maybe that's where I am. Maybe I'm not being dropped off at some nuthouse for girls who've tried to off themselves where I'll be forced to talk about the feelings I no longer have. Maybe my parents are taking me to the one place that can offer me salvation, an escape from the soulless redneck grind I've endured for so many years.

"Cams, sweetie," my mother interrupts. "We're here. Time to get out."

I blink, confused. But she's right. We've driven through

the gate somehow and are now parked in front of a huge Greek Revival home replete with looming columns and a vast wrap-around porch. My father opens the car door for me, but I rebuff his assistance and my mom's false cheer. I hate the way they're acting, like they're being strong for me, which I never asked for and never would. I don't ask anything of anyone.

There's no point in stalling, though. Plus, my parents look so hopeful, I don't have the heart to tell them that bringing me here is useless. So I haul myself out of the car and take a closer look at the building in front of me. On the porch, near the entryway, I spy wicker lounge furniture, potted canna lilies in full bloom, and glossy black shutters. *Very antebellum chic,* my mind whispers.

And yeah, I hate it.

Everything about it.

TWELVE

DANI

ON THE BRIEF TOUR we're offered, I check out everything. Even if I'm not interested, it's just how my brain works. I absorb information in case it might be needed, and it's an instinct that's served me well. If only for the opportunity to be proven right on more than one occasion, because what sweeter words exist in this language than "I told you so"?

But the more I look around, the more I learn, I can see in a way that this place is ingenious, designed as it is to give the illusion of freedom. Sitting on eighty acres of pristine wilderness, it comes complete with forest trails, a fishing pond, even a working barn and an organic garden project.

I'm informed that there are two residence halls, thirty-six

beds, and that clients are assigned to their rooms by age and level of care. Beyond the main administrative building, the other structures here are more modern, representing eco-friendly architecture, and the tour guide—a stern-faced, light-skinned woman who introduces herself simply as "Yolanda"—points out which buildings are used for group therapy, art therapy, food prep, yoga, and more. I don't track a lot of what she's saying, because even though the property is meant to exude openness and exploration, what jumps out are all the security measures. The way staff lingers in every shadow and every door requires a card or a code for both entry and exit.

"What about medical concerns?" my aunt asks.

"We have a state-of-the-art clinic that's housed in the main building," Yolanda says. "That's also where our admin offices are, and some of our therapists meet with clients in there as well."

"Are you a therapist?" I ask.

She turns to me. "I'm the head programming coordinator. I oversee most of the classes and activities that you'll engage in during your stay. I also work closely with both our clinical and medical staff to ensure that all of our clients' needs are being met."

"Did you go to school for that?"

"I have a background in education and leadership."

"So you're a teacher?"

"Not exactly."

"A doctor?"

"Is Christina available yet?" Aunt Bea has her phone out, checking the time, and Christina is her friend, the director, who was too busy to meet us when we first arrived.

"Let me find out." Yolanda leads us back to the main building and invites us to sit on the front porch while we wait.

Once we're alone, Aunt Bea looks at me. "How're you feeling?"

"Terrified," I say in a rare rush of honesty. "I don't belong in a place like this. I don't need to be locked up."

"But you don't want to go home."

"I don't want to go anywhere that treats me like a problem."

"You have some say in that, you know."

My eyes fill with tears. "Can't I stay with you? At your place? That's all I want. I'll go to school. I'll stay out of trouble."

"Sweetie," she says. "You know why that's not possible. I care about you very much. And I understand why living with my sister has been hard for you. But—" She holds a finger up to keep me from interrupting. "But we both know what was in your purse, and that's not a small problem. It's a real one, and it would not be responsible of me to ignore that or downplay how serious addiction can be."

"I'm *not* an addict."

My aunt sighs, then grabs her purse. "I'm going to have to speak with Christina later. I really need to get to the office. But,

Dani, I know this isn't easy. I'm very proud of you for taking this step, and I hope you see this as the gift it really is."

"It's two weeks, right? That's all? That's as long as I have to stay?"

"That depends on how you do," she says. "It's up to you."

"Can I stay at your place when I get out?" I ask.

Aunt Bea softens. "We'll see."

"There's nothing wrong with me, you know. I'm only doing this because my mom's making me. She can't ever admit she's wrong or not in control, and so she's punishing me for her own issues."

She sighs again. "Goodbye, Dani."

THIRTEEN

CAMILA

I'M IN MY ASSIGNED ROOM, lying on the twin bed closest to the window, when I hear a soft knock. I don't answer, but that knock is soon followed by the sound of a creaking door and the shuffling of shoes on bare wood.

"Hello?" a singsong voice says. "I'm coming in, so don't, like, freak out or anything."

I roll over and open my eyes. Trust me, freaking out's the last thing I plan on doing.

The girl—my new roommate, I'm guessing—standing in the doorway, paper bags full of clothing clutched in her arms, is not really what I expected. I've only been here myself for an hour or so, so what do I know? But the other girls I've caught glimpses of have all been pale and wide-eyed and radiating with tragedy in that way you see in movies sometimes.

But this girl is different. I sit up, rubbing my eyes, to get a better look. She's tall, Black, and there's nothing fragile or tragic about her. I watch the way she moves about the room, taking in the furniture, the view, my own meager belongings.

"I'm Camila," I say. "I just got here today, too."

The girl looks at me. "How do you spell that?"

"C-A-M-I-L-A."

"Huh." She drops the bags on the floor in a heap. "I'm Danielle. You can call me Dani, though. Most people do."

"Okay."

Dani paces the room, touching every surface as she passes by. The dresser, the door handle, the windowsill, the desk. "They've seriously got everything bolted down, huh?"

"That's the idea," I say.

"Hey, is that the bed you want?"

"The one I'm on?"

"Yeah."

"I don't know," I say. "I didn't really think about it. Why? Did you want it?"

She shrugs. "I like being near the window."

"Window doesn't open."

"But still."

"Fine. Take it." I slide out from under the sheets and walk to the bed by the closet.

"Are you pissed?" she asks.

"I don't care about the beds," I say.

"Okay, great." Dani flops down on the mattress I've gifted her. The one by the window. Then she promptly gets up again. *"Fuck."*

I shake my head. This girl is exhausting. So much movement. It's nonstop. There's definitely no body awareness or control going on with her. "What is it?"

"Can you believe they took our stuff? They took my whole *purse*. And my suitcase."

"What'd you have in there?" I ask. "We followed the packing list and supply guide the clinic sent over, and they didn't take anything. I didn't bring much, though."

Dani tightens her jaw. "Do you know where the bathroom is?"

"No one showed you where the bathroom was?"

"I said I could figure it out myself. Yolanda was telling me—"

"Who's Yolanda?" I ask.

"The programming coordinator."

"I don't think I met her."

"Anyway, she was telling me all about how she had to help get ready for lunch, and it's not like I need a babysitter to get around. I'm only here for a couple of weeks because my mom's a total control freak and thinks it'll help her reelection chances."

My eyelids flutter. "Reelection chances?"

Dani takes a step toward me, head cocked like a curious poodle. "You okay? They got you pretty drugged up, don't they?"

"I guess."

"How come?"

"I was in the hospital a while back. Then I did another program. I guess they think I need it. The medication, I mean."

She frowns. "Hospital? Why were you there?"

"I tried to kill myself," I say.

FOURTEEN

DANI

I STARE AT CAMILA, unsure of how to respond. I mean, first off, I didn't think anyone suicidal would be in a place like this. Isn't this meant to be a step up from those locked-ward places? Also, who just says things like that out loud? To a total *stranger*?

"Why would you do that?" I ask her. "Why would you want to be dead?"

Camila, who's this tiny brown-skinned girl with a squeaky Southern voice, considers my question carefully before answering. "I don't know why."

"You don't *know*?"

She reaches forward to hug her knees. "Well, first off, I'm a dancer. Dance is my whole life. I've been competing since I was in grade school, and recently I got accepted into this amazing dance academy that I've been applying to for years."

"Was it too much pressure?" I ask.

"No. That's not— See, my parents, they'd saved money to send me, but when I didn't get in after the second time I applied, they spent their savings on remodeling the house. I didn't tell them I was applying again, which was my fault, but they felt so bad about letting me down. . . ." She trails off.

"So they couldn't afford your dance school tuition but they can afford to send you here? Yeah, I hope you aren't falling for that story. Glad you didn't die for it."

Camila falters. "Doesn't insurance pay for this?"

"Fuck if I know," I say. "Maybe you're right. You want to go walk around? Yolanda said to come down and meet everyone when I was ready."

"Yolanda, the programming coordinator."

"You can probably just call her Yolanda."

"You really want to meet people?" Camila asks. "That's a thing you want to do?"

"What else would we do?"

"I don't know."

"Yeah, well, I'm not into sitting around and feeling sorry for myself. No offense," I add.

"None taken." She pauses, then: "Yeah, sure. Let's go. Might as well see what this place is like."

Camila fades once we make our way outside. It's like watching a flower wilt, the way she pulls into herself the moment we're in sunshine. On top of that, she looks utterly lost.

"They really let us just walk around?" she asks, sort of awe-struck. "On our own?"

"In a limited capacity," I tell her. "Apparently, we can move around this main courtyard during the day and access the treatment facilities. But the key cards tell them where we are at all times, and also they have cameras everywhere. A lot of staff, too. It's really a mirage of free will—not to be confused with actual freedom—but I guess that's better than *One Flew over the Cuckoo's Nest* or whatever."

"Oh."

"Didn't you get a tour earlier?" I ask.

She shakes her head.

"Well, allow me, then. I saw everything when I came in. My aunt, she knows the director, Christina something."

"Sánchez," Camila says. "Yeah, my parents and I met with her."

"What's she like?"

"I don't know. My parents had a lot of questions for her. They get super nervous about change and commitment. But she was fine, I guess."

"Is she Latina?"

"Yeah."

"Are you?"

Camila nods. "My dad's Colombian. He came here when he was eight. And my mom's parents are both from Juárez. But she grew up in Mississippi. In the heart of Dixie Alley."

"And you live here? In Georgia? That's wild."

"Where are you from?" she asks.

"Dallas."

"How'd you end up in Georgia?"

"That," I say, "is a long story."

"The town I live in is about two hours away. It's really rural and small. And depressing."

"Hey, what meds do they have you on?" I ask.

"I don't know. All my meds are from the doctor I saw back home."

"But what are they?"

Her recall is slow. "Um, an antidepressant, for sure. And a mood stabilizer. And something else. I forget what it's called. Seroquel, maybe? Sera something."

"Do they work?"

"No idea."

"Do you feel good?"

"I definitely don't feel good."

"Then how do you feel?"

"Empty," she says. "Like I'm not really here. Or I'm not meant to be."

We approach a small, ivy-draped building with white French doors open to a tiny French garden. Inside, I catch sight of a jumble of bodies, long hair, long legs. Someone waves to us. I don't know who.

"Think those are the other girls?" I ask Camila.

She shrugs and looks miserable, like someone sat on her puppy. Plus, she's doing the wilting thing again.

"Well, come on already." I grab her arm, pull her with me. "First impressions are everything."

FIFTEEN

CAMILA

DREAD GRIPS MY BONES as we enter into a sunroom that's wide and bright and filled with beanbag chairs and pillows. A ceiling fan with palm-frond paddles spins lazily above us, and there's a table set against the back wall that's draped with a white tablecloth and holds trays of fresh fruit and chilled jugs of tropical-looking juice.

There are also girls everywhere. Maybe half a dozen or so. They lounge atop the beanbags like a pride of lionesses, some talking, one sleeping. A redheaded girl is braiding another red-headed girl's hair. The rest are all blond.

I feel sick almost immediately. I shouldn't have come out

here, and I shouldn't have let Dani influence my judgment. There needs to be structure when it comes to acclimating to a new place. It's like learning choreography; you can't just jump in and expect to get it right. There's a process, *my* process, and this isn't it.

At all.

"Camila."

I glance up. Dani's gesturing for me to come closer. I obey, but something tells me that she's more comfortable among this pile of broken white girls than she is with me. I see it in the way she laughs with them, the way she takes up space. She's so confident. She's sure about who she is, which makes me wonder why she's here in the first place.

"This is my roommate, Camila," Dani says. "She's, like, a really amazing dancer."

The pride of girls lick their metaphoric paws and look me over and offer a tepid greeting before returning to Dani's orbit. She's quickly sucked into a conversation with a bubbly blond-haired girl, who it turns out used to live in Texas. I don't get the impression she's a fan—of the Lone Star State, that is—but I'm also too exhausted to care.

After a few moments, standing starts to feel awkward, and I sit on the floor, positioning myself a few feet away from the two girls involved in hair braiding.

They both notice me. I clock them looking up, running their gaze over my body, my face, before returning to their conversation. Well, the one getting her hair braided is doing the talking, soft murmuring about some friends back home. The other girl's absorbed in her task, coppery plaits gripped tight between her fingers as she pulls them rhythmically beneath each twist in a reverse-French style.

I focus on my fingernails, which are in need of trimming. How does that happen in a place like this? I'm sure I'm not allowed to have clippers. Maybe someone will do it for me. Like I'm an infant again, which I guess I am. Although I was unruly then, too, on account of my childhood eczema. I've seen photos of me as a baby with socks over my hands because I couldn't be trusted not to scratch myself bloody.

"What's your name?" a voice says.

I look up, and now both the girls are looking at me. I don't know how long they've been waiting for me to respond, but it's clear I've crossed the Rubicon of acceptable behavior. The braiding girl has her lip curled into a sneer, and the other appears on the verge of giggling.

A patter of helplessness rains down on me. I'm not sure how to respond, and I resent having to do anything at all. Out of the corner of my eye, I catch sight of my roommate holding court over the other girls. They're staring up at her, and she's got her head thrown back in laughter.

And well, you know what? I'm happy for her. I really am. In fact, she's so absorbed with her newfound status, she doesn't even notice as I rise to my feet and head for the door. As I leave the building, I can hear Dani's voice rise above the others.

"Hey, so what meds are you all taking?" she asks.

Once outside, my driving urge is to be left alone, and when I see a door marked *Library*, it's a no-brainer to slip inside using my key card. The room's empty, which feels weird, but the system knows where I am and maybe that's enough. It's a large space, though, with rows of books running along the wall, and there are tables in the middle of the room and a few worn armchairs. One table, however, has two computers. There's a sign-up sheet for both, which gives me the sense that they're often in high demand. But at the moment, I'm the only one here.

Plopping myself down in front of one of the Macs, I use the mouse to wake it up. Laminated instructions for logging on— *System will shut down after 20 minutes! Save your work!*—are taped to the screen, along with stern warnings about moderated content and protected browsing, but once I'm online, I'm able to pull up my email. There's a lot, actually. More than I expected. I've only been able to get online once since getting out of the ER, since that Dalton program made my parents take my phone. Anyway, I ignore all the messages from people from my high school. They all have subject lines like "Camila!" and "Thinking of you" and "Oh nooooo ☹☹☹," which makes me feel more suicidal than ever, and I delete them in one fell swoop. None of these people know or care about me, and there's nothing honest about their words. There's nothing honest about anyone; we're all looking out for our own self-interest, all the time, and I just wish people could be honest about that.

There's also a message from Ivan, and that one I do open.

Dear Cams,

I don't know what to say, but I don't want that to keep me from telling you how much I care for you and how much I'm rooting for you to get better. You're a special person, Cams. I know I'm not always very open or talkative about anything deep, but I think you know how much your friendship means to me.

I'm here. Anytime you need anything, I'm here for you. Okay?

—I

My eyes sting, and I hit delete as fast as I can. Stupid. It was stupid of me to open that. I don't want anyone's pity, and I haven't asked for it, either.

Then I spy the message I've been looking for.

Dear Camila,

Congratulations again on your acceptance into our program. We hope you are seriously considering Fieldbrook as a place to continue developing your incredible talent in the field of dance. This is a reminder that your admissions decision and $500 deposit must be received by May 30 of this year in order to reserve your spot. If you have any question, please do not hesitate to contact us. We look forward to seeing you on campus next fall!

Sincerely,

Laura Villanova, Vice President of Admissions

I read the letter, then read it again, and the urge is there to delete it, too. To get rid of any evidence of what is both the greatest achievement and greatest failure of my life.

But I don't.

SIXTEEN

DANI

THE NOVELTY OF this place is fading fast. First of all, I have nothing to do and no one to do it with. After that fruit and juice break, all the girls got up and told me they had somewhere to go. And they weren't even going to the same place. The ones I asked described some variety of individual or group therapy sessions. I didn't even understand half of what they were talking about— EMDR and CBT and DBT. It all sounds made up. But the point is that they're gone, and somehow my roommate's gone, too.

It's just me.

I lounge around on the beanbags for a while, staring up at that swirling ceiling fan. It kind of reminds me of this party I went to last year with my cousin Abe and some of his friends before he left for Hollywood. We drove to Oklahoma and stayed on this property one of his buddies was renting that edged up on this huge wildlife preserve. The cabin was beyond rustic—all smoke-stained walls and full of these disgusting jumping spiders—but it had a fan just like this one. When I woke up Sunday morning with the worst hangover of my life, my solution was to smoke a joint, take a little Addy, and just stare up at that fan until my head felt stable again.

Yeah, well, it's not giving me any stability now, and I could definitely go for some Addy. That's not an addict talking, though. I'm just being realistic, since I don't know how the hell I'm expected to have any sort of motivation in a place like this. I'm not a touchy-feely, emotion-oriented kind of person; I'm a thinker. A doer. A problem solver. My mom's the same way, actually, which is part of why we clash.

My head throbs at the thought of my mom, but this also gives me a sudden spark of an idea. Leaping to my feet, I nearly trip over the beanbags like a circus clown in my hurry to get to the door.

Back out on the main lawn, muggy air pulls sweat down my back as I march toward the main administrative building and ring the access bell. Once I'm buzzed in, the woman seated at the front desk smiles and asks how she can help me.

"Is there an infirmary here?"

She keeps smiling. "What it is you need?"

"I don't feel good," I say. "My head hurts. My stomach hurts, too. It's bad."

"Okay."

"Well, I wanted to see about getting some medicine. There's gotta be like a nurse's office, right?"

"What kind of medicine?" she asks. "Something your doctor's prescribed?"

"I don't know what kind. I don't have a doctor. Not here, at least. I do back in Texas, but he doesn't know I'm here."

She pauses. "Well, I think Dr. Allegheny's on duty for another hour. You're welcome to head back to our care clinic and see if he's free. Only our medical staff is able to dispense medication to residents. That's not something I can do."

"What about aspirin?"

"That's a medicine," she says briskly.

I follow her directions down the main corridor and up a flight of stairs to the so-called care clinic. It's like walking into an actual doctor's office, with a tidy waiting room and at least four separate exam rooms. Two of the doors are closed.

I approach the only person I see: an older bearded Black man who's wearing a rumpled gray suit and a red paisley tie and what look like honey-yellow Crocs while working at a standing desk and typing on a keyboard.

"Dr. Allegheny?" I ask.

He gives a quick nod.

"I was told to come talk to you. My name's Danielle. I just got here today."

He's still typing. "Welcome, Danielle."

"They said I could come and ask you."

"Ask me what?"

"My head hurts, and I don't feel very good. I was wondering if you had anything you could give me?"

Dr. Allegheny bobs his head, and I can't read his expression under that scruffy beard of his, but when he finishes typing, he steps back and gestures toward an open exam room. "Why don't we go in there."

I nod and follow, and he offers me an armchair while he maneuvers around his desk in that bumbling way boomers do, and I guess this isn't going to be a medical exam, which is a relief. Only, now Dr. Allegheny is on a different computer, typing away again, while he tells me to expand on what's bothering me.

"It's my head," I repeat. "That's the main thing. But also, it's a little weird being here. I feel stressed, you know. Or anxious."

He glances up. "Do you often feel anxious?"

"I don't know." I tap my fingers on the desk, let my knee jiggle around. "No. Maybe. It's hard for me to sleep sometimes."

"How long has your head been hurting?"

"When has it not?" I quip.

Dr. Allegheny lifts an eyebrow. A bushy one.

I sigh. "Since this morning."

"When did you last eat?"

"My aunt and I stopped at Panera on the way up here. God, that was early. Like, nine in the morning, maybe? I had a breakfast sandwich. On a brioche, not the ciabatta."

"It's now four in the afternoon," he says.

"Point taken."

"Well, I suggest you get some food soon. Other than that, I can write out an order for you for some acetaminophen. Or ibuprofen, if you prefer."

"An order?"

"That's how we dispense medication here."

"What about something for sleeping? The anxiety, you know?"

He's back on the computer. "We can talk about that tomorrow. You have an appointment with me at ten a.m. Although not here. We'll meet in my office on the third floor. Suite 302."

"Why am I seeing you tomorrow?"

Dr. Allegheny clasps his hands together, and this is when he finally, *finally* gives me his full attention. "I'm going to be your psychiatrist during your time here at Peach Tree Hills. We'll meet tomorrow to discuss your goals and how I can help support you in reaching them. We can assess your other concerns as well."

I frown. "I thought you were a medical doctor."

"I am a medical doctor." Fingers still clasped, he jams his

thumbs beneath his chin and gazes at me with all the manu-factured patience of a school administrator.

"Well, you don't seem too interested in my medical concerns."

"What makes you think I'm not interested?"

"The fact that you won't help me!"

"I have offered you help, Danielle. You've described for me that you've had a headache since arriving here at Peach Tree Hills early this afternoon. You also noted that you have trouble sleep-ing on occasion and that you've been feeling stressed and anx-ious about coming here. My medical suggestion is that you take acetaminophen for the headache accompanied with a snack to get your blood sugar up. The trouble sleeping is unsurprising, given this transition and the upheaval in your life. However, to remedy your concern, I would suggest you practice rigorous sleep hygiene, which includes avoiding screens or television for at least an hour before bedtime and only using your bed for sleep activities."

"As opposed to what?" I ask warily.

"Anything else." He slides a pamphlet across his desk at me. The title reads *How to Improve Your Relationship with Sleep* and the accompanying photo of a girl lying in bed with a sleep mask is equal parts alarming and pathetic.

"None of this is going to help me," I say.

"What would you suggest?" he asks.

"Well, I've used Ambien before."

"For sleep problems?"

"What else?"

He leans back. "You tell me."

"I don't like what you're implying," I snap. "I'm not clueless, you know. I can read subtext."

"I definitely don't think you're clueless, Danielle."

"But I'm a sixteen-year-old girl who's come to you, a doctor, a grown adult man, asking for help. And instead you insist on treating me with suspicion and spite and all these leading questions meant to trip me up. It's beyond offensive, and you'd better believe I'm going to tell everyone I can how you've treated me and how unfair it is." My words spill out of me, hot and angry, filling the space between us. Then I pause, waiting for him to back down the way people always do when you call them on their bullshit.

Dr. Allegheny nods slowly. "I think I understand what you're saying. You're frustrated with me, and it feels unfair that you have to ask me for what you've been able to get on your own in the past, and you'd like to me to know that you prefer to make decisions for yourself. Do I have that right?"

I nod. Breathe a sigh of relief. He gets it.

"Is there anything else you'd like for me to know?"

My lips twitch in victory. "That's it."

"Okay, then." He scribbles something on a prescription pad before tearing it off and handing it to me. "Why don't you go ahead and take this to Marcia at the front desk. She'll make sure it gets filled at mealtime."

"Thanks." I look down. "Wait, this is for *Tylenol*?"

He blinks all innocently. "Isn't that what we discussed?"

"Yes, but—"

Dr. Allegheny holds up a hand. "I'm afraid that's all we have time for today, Danielle. We'll talk more tomorrow at our regular meeting time. It sounds like you have a lot on your mind, and I'm really looking forward to working with you."

I snort. "You are?"

"Oh yes," he says with the broadest of smiles. "I most definitely am."

SEVENTEEN

CAMILA

"SWEETIE. HON. What're you doing?"

I blink, look up. A short woman with pink lipstick and a collared *Staff* shirt tucked into a neat pair of khakis is smiling at me. She's got a thick mane of dark curly hair that falls past her shoulders, and her eyes are framed by ruby-red cat-eye glasses.

"I'm sitting," I tell her, which is true. After checking my email, I came out here to the courtyard and sat on the stone wall across from the yoga studio. Not for any reason, exactly. I just didn't know where else to go.

"How are you feeling?" the woman asks me. "I'm Yolanda, by the way. We didn't get a chance to meet earlier, but I'm one of the staff directors."

I look at her. "I'm Camila."

"Do you know where you're supposed to be right now?"

"I'm supposed to be somewhere?"

"All our guests have a full schedule that includes therapy, group process, art, exercise, and, if it's part of your treatment plan, schoolwork."

"I didn't get one of those. A plan."

"Then I'm sure you'll learn more tomorrow after you meet with your care team."

"Okay," I say, but Yolanda doesn't move. She just stands there, smiling at me.

Finally: "We usually prefer that our A-level guests don't wander too much."

"What's A-level?" I ask.

She reaches to pat my arm. "It's fine for you to be out here. It's important to get some fresh air and sunlight. But from here on out, we'll need for you to check in with us about your whereabouts."

My cheeks warm. "But I didn't *know*."

"I said it was fine, hon. And later, when your team agrees, you'll be able to do a lot more. We have equine therapy available at the barn. Do you like horses?"

"It doesn't sound like it's fine." My voice comes out whinier than I intend. "It sounds like I've done something wrong and you just don't want to say it."

"Camila, I can ensure you that's not—"

"Everything's a secret around here, and I hate it!"

"Hey, hey." The woman—Yolanda—sits beside me. "It's all right. I told you that."

I shake my head, lip trembling, as my eyes fill with tears I have no use for. It's embarrassing. Worse, it's humiliating.

"Well, look," she says. "It's just about dinnertime now. We eat at six on the patio. It's family style, and I think you'll find the food is really delicious. I'm a terrible cook, so I try and eat here as often as I can. Why don't I show you where everyone is? Would that be okay?"

I nod, wipe my cheeks.

Yolanda stands, brushes off her khakis, and beckons for me to follow. We walk back through the main courtyard and past the two residence halls. Just beyond, nestled among a copse of pine trees, is the kitchen and dining area. Just adjacent is a brick-paved patio dotted with three picnic tables crowded with girls and staff.

"You eat outside?" I ask.

"When we can," she says, and my pulse skyrockets because I don't know what the rules are for eating outside or family style or where I'm supposed to sit. Plus, everyone is already eating and passing food around, and my legs go weak because how do people just *do* this?

"Camila!"

My head snaps up. It's my roommate, Dani. She's grinning and waving at me from one of the tables.

I wave back.

"Come sit with me!" She edges her butt closer to the girl beside her, exposing a small space that I guess I could fit in. I glance at Yolanda, who nods for me to go.

"Thanks," I tell Dani, sliding onto the bench and doing my best not to let our legs touch.

"Sure thing." My roommate hands me a paper plate and spork as I unfold a napkin—I'm somehow entrusted with an actual cloth one—and place it in my lap. Then I look around. I recognize a few faces, but that's it. So much is happening all around me. There's the passing of food, the murmuring of voices, and even the purpling haze of twilight that's come down to soften all our edges.

A strange, detached part of me can appreciate the harmony of this scene, the near-painful beauty of picnic tables bearing red-checkered cloths, and the way everything's lit up by strands of tiny lights strung above us, crisscrossing the patio and weaving through a wooden pergola that's also lined with honeysuckle and twisting jasmine. It's perfect in this heartbreaking kind of way, but the truth is that the rest of me can't stand it. Any of it. I can't stand being here.

I just *can't.*

I hold my breath and wait until Danielle starts talking with another girl, absorbed in a conversation full of light and curiosity and everything good. Then, when I know she can't stop me, I get up and go.

EIGHTEEN

DANI

UGH. I DRAG MYSELF down the dorm hallway, and could this day get any crappier? Not only did that meeting with the doctor blow up in my face, but now I have to deal with my hot mess of a roommate. I mean, I *know* the counselors went and talked to her after her dinner freak-out, but I'm the one who has to live with her.

Fucking hell.

I knock on the door when I reach our room. It's eight p.m. and this is when we all get locked inside, although we're allowed to gather in the first-floor lounge until ten, which is room curfew and lights-out.

I knock again when there's no answer, then push the

door open, stepping into the room slowly. "Camila? I'm coming in."

The lights are off, but I can see her clear as day, thanks to moonlight spilling through the bedroom window and hitting the opposite wall. My roommate's curled on her bed like a dead prawn, just like she was when I first got here. I switch on the overhead light.

"What's going on?" I ask. Camila's dark hair is wet, and she's changed out of her earlier shorts and performance tee into a pair of fleecy long-sleeved sweats. "Jesus. Aren't you hot? The AC sucks in this place."

"No," she says flatly. "I'm not hot."

I sit on my bed and face her. "Are you okay?"

"Yes."

"You sure?"

"I said yes."

"Very convincing," I say. "Oh, by the way, the nurse on duty tonight said she'll be coming up soon with medication, in case you're expecting anything. Then it's curfew or whatever. We have to stay in here like inmates until six a.m. Can you believe that shit?"

Camila's eyes widen. "Someone's coming *here*?"

"That's literally what I just said."

Suddenly Camila's sitting up, acting all aggravated. "She won't check our room or anything, will she? They can't go through our stuff? Legally, I mean."

"They didn't say anything about that." I bend down to pull off my shoes. Then a smile creeps across my face. "Hey, what're you hiding anyway? Something good? I thought they already went through your stuff."

Camila looks at me.

"You're clearly worried about them finding something," I tell her.

"I didn't say that."

"It doesn't bother me. I just want to know what it is. If it's something that, you know, I might enjoy, too."

"Hold up," Camila says. "Is *that* why you're here? Because of *drugs*?"

Now my shoulders tense. "What're you talking about?"

"That's it, isn't it? You're here for drug treatment. Detox or something like that?"

"You're saying you think I'm a drug addict?"

She shrugs. "I don't care. But it's the only thing that makes sense since it doesn't seem like you're having a mental health breakdown like the rest of us."

"Maybe I just hide my mental breakdowns really well," I tell her.

"Maybe," she admits. "But I—"

She's interrupted by a sharp knock on the door. We both turn and watch as the night nurse enters, all drug-dealer style, carrying her carefully labeled stash and a big bottle of water. No drugs for me, obviously, since I was already gifted Dr. Allegheny's super-generous Tylenol at dinner. Anyway, I'm not in the mood to sit around and watch Camila swallow her Xanax. Grabbing my towel, I jump up and head for the bathroom.

"Hold on," the nurse says to me.

I stop. "What?"

"There's a phone call for you."

"Where? From who?"

"Go to room 101. You can use the phone there."

NINETEEN

CAMILA

EVEN THOUGH I didn't want her here, I feel worse once the nurse leaves. The pills aren't sitting right, and even though I don't actually think I'll get sick, I can't stop thinking about the fact that I *could*. Then what would I do? Doubt leaves me clammier, and finally, I flip off the lights and crawl under the covers to try and force myself to sleep.

It's useless. I kick at the sheets. The walls are paper-thin, and through them, I hear running water and laughter and music and even pounding footsteps. It's as if what I've always known is true; that everyone's hanging out together, gathering in some unknown spot they all instinctively gravitate toward, while in here I'm alone. It feels worse even than being in that Dalton hospital's day treatment program, since there wasn't anything you could be excluded from in that place, other than the morgue. Not to mention I was so heavily sedated the first few days that I could barely keep my eyes open, much less make friends. Not that I wanted to, and I still don't want to, but it doesn't feel great knowing that I don't fit in.

A whimper escapes me, my mind flashing back to the moment I swallowed those pills by the riverside. It felt good to do it. It felt so damn good, which I know I'm not supposed to admit. No one's ever supposed to admit that.

But it did. In that moment, my heart had shimmered and warmed in a way that was rare and special and mine because I'd done it. I'd won. I'd found a way to beat back the emptiness, to crawl from the pit of despair that I'd danced my way into.

My last thought as I lay in the grass to die was of the loneliest whale. I'd once read about this poor pitiful creature whose vocalizations came out at the wrong frequency for other whales to pick up. As a result, it had spent its life alone, swimming the depths of the ocean and crying out for companionship it would never find. That story was just about the saddest thing I'd ever encountered, and so that made me happy, too, knowing that in the afterlife I'd never again have my soul crushed by a whale.

Slipping one hand beneath my mattress, I dig around for what I've hidden there—a tiny set of travel tweezers that I stole from my mother's purse on the ride down. I got them inside by burying them deep in the rubber soles of my running shoes, which no one bothered to inspect once the laces were removed.

I pluck the tool from the mattress coils and swiftly slide it under my shirt, pressing the thin metal ends up against my flank. It's a crude attack. The tweezers are almost weightless, that's how small they are, and I adjust, gripping them in my fist so that I can scrape and drag, my knuckles straining with effort as I push down harder, until finally, finally, my flesh gives way. I yelp, then eagerly reach with my fingers for the puncture spot. It's warm, sticky, and I gird myself to go again when I hear the faint creak of the doorknob.

Whipping my hand back out and shoving the tweezers away in the darkness, I freeze, listening intently as Dani creeps in without saying a word. She can be quiet, too, I guess. But something about her presence feels different, even in the way she tiptoes across the wood floor, careful not to wake me.

"Hey," I whisper so as not to startle her. "Are you okay?"

She doesn't turn to look at me. "I guess."

"Who was it? On the phone?"

Dani's silent for a moment. "It was my parents. I hadn't talked to them in, like, a week, and they insisted on hearing my voice."

"A week?"

"It's a long story." She sounds exhausted. Sad, maybe, too.

"Well," I say. "I'm sorry if it was a hard conversation or

whatever. I know those aren't easy."

She starts sliding off her jeans, pulling on a pair of sleep shorts. "There's one upshot at least."

"What's that?"

"I'll have something to talk about in therapy tomorrow."

I smile.

Across the room, bathed in moonlight, Dani pulls her hair back, then slides beneath the covers.

"Hey, Camila," she whispers.

"Yeah?"

"Thanks for asking if I was okay."

TWENTY

DANI

"SO WHAT'RE WE supposed to talk about?" I'm sitting in Dr. Allegheny's office—not in the medical clinic, but on the third floor—and it's super stiff and formal, just like how I imagined. No medical stuff; just brown leather and dark wood. I bet he's got a bottle of bourbon hidden in a drawer somewhere.

"How did you sleep last night?" he asks, and it feels weird, not like yesterday, because we're both sitting in club chairs with no desk between us.

"Is that like a therapist thing?" I reply. "Answering a question with a question?"

"Probably," he concedes. "But it's not a good habit. I apologize."

I pull my legs into the leather chair I'm sitting in. "It just feels a little cliché, you know? Like you're getting ready to ask me about my mother."

"Should I be asking about your mother?"

"Probably."

Dr. Allegheny smooths his cardigan. "Well, we can talk about anything you'd like to talk about in here. But I did want to go over your treatment plan at Peach Tree Hills. I wanted to get your input and also gather some more information."

"Aren't you going to tell me who you are?" I ask. "You're a total stranger."

He sits back and smiles in a way that makes the lines around his eyes crinkle. It's odd, how he's so fatherly but also not like my father at all. "Of course. I'm a psychiatrist who specializes in working with adolescents and young adults. I've been in practice for thirty-five years, and I've worked or consulted with Peach Tree Hills for the last twelve. I still have my own practice in the Atlanta area, where I specialize in complex trauma and mood disorders."

"Are there are a lot of Black psychiatrists?"

"I'm not the only one in the field, if that's what you're asking. But no, there aren't a lot, unfortunately. Although that may be changing."

"That's what everyone says, and nothing ever does change."

"Fair enough. Well, as a psychiatrist, that means I'm an MD and can prescribe medication. But I'm also trained in psychotherapy, and what I enjoy about working here is that I have the opportunity to do talk therapy with my clients, which I feel can be very effective in most cases. I tend to approach therapy through a social-justice lens that's both strength-based and humanistic."

"Am I supposed to know what that means?"

"It means that I don't believe I have the answers—you're the expert in your own life—but I see my role as being someone who can help you sort out some of the conflicts you've been experiencing. Perhaps your understanding of how the world works is in flux, or perhaps the environment you're in isn't a healthy one for you for some reason."

"This is giving me a headache," I tell him. "Another one."

"Did the Tylenol help?"

"I told you it wouldn't."

"I know you were upset with me about that."

"I was." I lift my chin. "I didn't like how you were talking to me. It felt like you wanted to punish me or prove a point."

"Punish you for what?"

"Needing help. Where's the social-justice lens in that?"

He nods. "It sounds like you appreciate honesty and direct communication."

"That's right."

"Then let's talk about why you're here and how that might impact our work together. You see, one of the reasons substance-use disorders can be so complex to treat is because they often co-occur with other mental health diagnoses. Some of those diagnoses might typically be treated with medication. However, the presence of a substance-abuse history makes this contraindicated in most cases. We don't want to replace dependence on one substance with another."

"I'm not dependent on anything!"

"Based on the information provided by your aunt and parents, it sounds like you've been using various substances, including alcohol, for a while now and—more importantly—that this usage has been having a negative impact on your life."

The back of my neck warms. "Of *course* that's what my parents would say. From their perspective, I'm always the problem. It's always me. It's what they say to keep from having to acknowledge what's wrong with them. They're the negative impact, you know."

"Well, your aunt reported finding methamphetamine, alcohol, Xanax, and Provigil in your purse, along with a few other substances that she couldn't identify."

I'm beyond exasperated. "I didn't say I don't use the occasional substance every now and then. Just that I'm not an addict."

"Okay."

"Fuck you," I snarl. "I'm not the problem, and I never have been. I'm the scapegoat in my family. For everything. Because they're perfect. My mom's perfect. And nothing will take that away from them."

"Do you think it's possible that both could be true at once?" he asks.

"What do you mean?"

"Is it possible that, yes, your parents are screwed up and seek to use you as the identified problem as a way to keep from addressing their own problems—and also that in using drugs and drinking to cope with your family's dysfunction, you've gotten stuck in your own cycle of self-destruction?"

I fold my arms. "That doesn't sound like me at all."

"Then how would you describe your role in your family's dynamic?"

"My parents called here last night," I tell him. "To talk to me. Did you know that? They were pretending that they were checking up on me and making sure I was safe, but their whole approach was so condescending. Like they wanted me to know how bad they felt that I had to be stuck in this place. My mom might as well have just said, 'I told you so.'"

Dr. Allegheny doesn't miss a beat. "And what was that like for you to hear?"

I sigh. Loudly. "You want to know what my role is in our family?"

"Yes. I do."

"It's helping them to see what hypocrites they are. Someone has to be honest and tell the truth, and that's what I do. But no good deed and shot messengers and all."

"It sounds like it was a difficult phone call."

I flop back in the chair. "It was fine. I don't expect you to throw me a fucking pity party."

"You know, in here, with me, it doesn't have to be," he says gently.

My eyes narrow. "It doesn't have to be what?"

"Fine," he tells me.

TWENTY-ONE

CAMILA

"I DON'T KNOW what I'm doing here," I tell the perky white woman sitting across from me. She's introduced herself as Dr. Roberts, and apparently, she's my new psychiatrist. My new therapist, too, which is different, since I thought psychiatrists just gave out meds. So far, however, all she's done is ask questions about suicide and self-harm and safety planning. All of which I've answered before.

"What do you mean?" she asks.

"I mean I don't get what the point of all this is."

"Of being in this room? Or you don't get the point of being here at Peach Tree Hills in the first place?"

I don't answer. It's not that her questions confuse or

confound me. They just don't feel necessary. I'll either hurt myself or I won't. Talking about it certainly doesn't feel like a deterrent. Worse, it feels like a trap. Plus, there's so much effort that comes with forming words and thoughts meant for someone else's consumption. I'm also really caught up with what Dr. Roberts looks like and what she's wearing. She's so young. The doctors I saw in the Dalton facility were all old and stuffy, with thin, papery skin and spatters of cafeteria food dotting their white coats. Dr. Roberts is wearing *yoga pants*. She's also got this stylish copper bob, red lipstick, and a smattering of freckles across the bridge of her nose.

"Camila?" She crosses her legs, leaning forward in her black office chair.

"I don't know," I say at last.

"Are you feeling okay? You look a little pale."

This would make sense, considering I literally came here after getting my blood drawn. But I just shrug and close my eyes, and before I know what's happening, Dr. Roberts is having me lie back in the chair while she wraps my arm in a blood pressure cuff.

"What's wrong?" I ask.

She pulls the cuff off. "Have you eaten today?"

"I went to breakfast." My memory's hazy, but I remember being served a plate of something hot. There was herbal tea, but no coffee. "I had fruit."

Dr. Roberts gets up and walks across the room. Her strides are brisk, businesslike. She reaches up on the toes of her Fly London heels and rummages in a cabinet for a meal replacement shake. She walks back, hands it to me, and waits until I sip at it before settling back into her chair. "How're you adjusting to your medication?"

"I don't know what to compare it to. I'm tired all the time. Queasy, too. Nothing tastes good, and I feel pretty out of it."

"How's your anxiety?"

"About the same."

"Are you sleeping?"

I nod. "I think so."

"Have you ever been to therapy, Camila?"

"No."

"You said earlier that you didn't understand why you were here."

I swallow more of the shake. "That's right."

"Well, Peach Tree Hills allows you to engage in your treatment process while living in a safe environment that's removed from all the regular stressors of your everyday life."

"I don't think my life back home is all that stressful."

"Did you want to come here?"

"No one asked me what I wanted."

"I see."

"I think it was the staff at the partial hospitalization

program who recommended that I come here. To my parents, obviously. I didn't think they'd say yes because . . ."

"Because why?" she asks.

"Because it's expensive." I look over at Dr. Roberts. "Right?"

"Is money a concern for you?"

"I don't know." I look up from the drink she gave me. My stomach's knotting with a sudden wave of guilt because I shouldn't be saying these things. I shouldn't even be thinking them.

"What was the partial hospitalization program like?" she asks.

I shake my head. "Different."

"In what way?"

"There were just a lot of rules, and the things we did were pretty repetitive. It mostly felt like structure for structure's sake. Here we can make choices. Or we're supposed to *feel* like we can make choices. Even though we're really only allowed to make the right ones."

"That doesn't sound like a choice."

"I guess not," I say.

"Any other differences?"

"I have a roommate," I manage to squeak. "That's, uh, new for me."

Dr. Roberts perks up. "What's that been like?"

"It's not the worst thing I've been through."

A smiles flashes across her face before vanishing. I sit

up a little and fold my hands neatly. Await her next question.

"My inquiry stands," she says. "How has it been getting to know your roommate?"

"Well, I don't *know her* know her. We only met yesterday. But she's not what I expected."

"What did you expect her to be?"

"Like me," I say.

"And what are you like?"

I roll my shoulders. "I don't know. Quiet, maybe. Or intense. Sad, I guess, and out of it. But Danielle's really bold and confident. Like I said, nothing like me at all."

"Are those qualities you admire? Boldness and confidence?"

"No. They're fine, I guess. Just not for me."

"Tell me about your history with friendships," Dr. Roberts urges.

"Like who my friends are?"

"Who or what the word means to you. Any of it."

"It doesn't *mean* anything to me. But I'm not someone who needs a lot of friends. It's not a very rewarding concept."

"Say more about that."

The shake must be hitting my bloodstream, because suddenly I do say more. I want to explain what I mean. "I just think some people really enjoy the whole back-and-forth that comes with being a friend. Knowing they're there when you need them and that they'll be loyal if you have a problem. But loyalty, knowing they'll be there, none of that's important to me. I don't mind talking with people and spending time with them, but I don't . . ."

"You don't what?"

"I don't want people depending on me. I'm just not the person who's going to drop everything and take care of someone because they got dumped by their boyfriend or their parents got divorced or whatever. It's not me."

"It sounds like having people depend on you is uncomfortable."

"Not uncomfortable," I say. "It's undesirable."

"What's the difference?"

"Well, *discomfort* makes it sound like a bad thing. Like it's a problem that I need to get over. But I don't think friendship is bad. I'm not saying that. And I don't think people depending on your support is bad, either. It's just not *my* preference. Like, no, I don't want Pepsi if I ordered a Coke. I just want the Coke."

She laughs. "So who's the Coke in this analogy?"

"My independence?"

"So *that's* what's really important to you."

"It's everything," I say.

"What about when you need support? Is there anyone you can go to?"

I wrinkle my nose. "Why would I need to go to anyone?"

"For connection. For help. For understanding."

I set the shake bottle down. There's still over half of it left, but it's too sweet for me to drink any more. "If I were to make friends with people just so they could be there when I needed them, wouldn't that be self-serving? It's like collecting a friend to put inside my emotional piggy bank. 'In case of emergency, be nice.'"

Dr. Roberts nods. "That's actually a really interesting metaphor. The piggy bank as friendship. Do you feel as if all friendships are transactional?"

"Don't you?" I ask.

"I suppose I can conceive of certain relationships as being transactional. Maybe even the one we have here, because it has boundaries and a set purpose and is mostly one way. But this is therapy, and to me, the word *friendship* implies something different." She pauses. "I know I'm repeating myself, but you didn't answer earlier. Is there anyone in your life that you feel you can go to for support?"

I lift my chin. "Me."

"Is that enough?"

"Is that a trick question?"

Dr. Roberts's eyes widen. "It's not meant to be."

"Look, what's wrong with my life has nothing to do with my approach to friendship. Or whether I do or don't need other people."

"Then what is wrong with your life?" she asks.

Only I don't answer. I'm too tired all of a sudden. Drained. "Can we talk about this next time? I don't feel very good."

Dr. Roberts glances at her watch. "That's fine, Camila. We'll meet again on Friday. Same time, okay?"

I nod.

"I'm also going to up your Zoloft dosage to help with your anxiety. And I'll prescribe a sedative for bedtime to help you sleep. Your body's still healing. Rest is very important. Same with nutrition." She gestures at the meal replacement shake.

"Okay," I say.

Dr. Roberts smiles. "I appreciate your coming to talk with me today, Camila. I know it can be hard, answering a lot of the same questions over and over, but that's how we can tell if your symptoms are improving and where you are in the treatment process. But if you have concerns about anything that's going on or anything we're doing, I hope that you'll feel comfortable enough to ask me. It's what I'm here for, and I really look forward to working with you."

I smile back as I get up to leave, but I don't return the niceties or confer any budding warmth or trust between us. Of course, *she's* going to say stuff like that to try and make me like her, and of course it's the kind of trick that's easy to see through, although I don't begrudge the effort. That's her job, after all. I'd do it, too, if it got me what I wanted in life.

But it won't.

TWENTY-TWO

DANI

I LEAVE DR. A'S OFFICE with a full schedule of my daily activities. Some of it I've seen before, like when we have to be in our rooms at night and what time we have to get up for breakfast and under what circumstances we're allowed to be alone or outside without supervision (almost none).

My day, however, looks exhausting. In the next fifteen minutes, I'm scheduled to complete an "intake assessment," whatever that is, and whatever that is will take over an hour. This is followed by lunch, something alarmingly titled "Ecotherapy—Finding Joy in the Garden," a group therapy session, and, finally, an academic assessment, which is penciled in to take at least *two hours*. Christ. Later comes dinner, and after that, a movie will be shown in the residential common lounge—something I've never heard of, but it features Meg Ryan, which isn't exactly promising.

I walk back down the stairs to the front reception area of the administrative building and ask about my intake thing. The woman smiles and leads me to a separate room, where an ancient laptop sits on a conference table. After waking it up, she types in a password and pulls up a program I don't recognize.

"How old is this computer?" I ask.

"I don't know."

"It looks like it weighs thirty pounds."

"That's unlikely."

"Is it running on Windows 7?"

"Have a seat," she says firmly. "You should be all set. "

"But what am I supposed to be doing?"

"You'll just answer some questions as they come up on the screen, and they'll be recorded and scored. You'll go over the results with one of the clinicians tomorrow. It's pretty self-explanatory, but if you have any questions, please don't hesitate to ask."

"Is it really going to take a full hour?"

"That depends on how quickly you get through it. There are about three hundred questions. Multiple choice."

I groan. "That's longer than the PSAT. You realize that, right?"

"No math questions, though."

"Will it make me a National Merit Scholar?"

She smiles. "Do you need water or anything to drink?"

"Got any Wild Turkey?" I ask.

The smile vanishes. "Let me know when you're done."

I settle into the chair and take a look at the computer screen, which reads:

```
            Welcome to the
    COHEN ALCOHOL AND DRUG ASSESSMENT
         FOR ADOLESCENTS — 2
              (CADAFA2)
```

Oh hell. After some exploratory scrolling, it's clear I'm intended to answer three hundred multiple-choice questions that are not only about my own personal history with drugs and alcohol, but also about my input on a bunch of annoying topics.

```
Exhibit A:
15.) In your opinion, what percentage
of United States high school students
consume at least one alcoholic beverage
in a given week?
     a. 0 — 10%
     b. 11 — 50%
     c. 51 — 75%
     d. 76% or higher
```

Well, this is basically the worst thing I've ever seen, and I once sat through an entire church production of *The Incredible Mr. Limpet*, a musical in which a fish—who used to be a man, mind you—is partially responsible for ending World War II.

Swiveling around in my chair, I take note of the fact that, although I'm alone in the conference room, the door's been left open. No card or code is needed for my departure. This feels fortuitous. Like an invitation, really.

Through the windows, dappled sunlight and blooming flowers conspire to tempt me. A few covert glances at the ceiling and walls don't reveal any cameras. This clinches it. Who wouldn't choose joy in the garden over this bullshit?

And with that, I push my chair back, slip from the room, and leave.

Once outside, I cruise the perimeter of the property, careful to stay out of sight and close to the tree line. I hate the niggle of paranoia my actions require. It feels as if I'm some kind of criminal when all I've done is reclaim my time. Isn't that part of my treatment plan? Figuring out who I am and what I want and how to understand myself better? Moving toward a more authentic life, as my mother would say.

My father, on the other hand, hates platitudes like that, and

I'm pretty much in agreement with him. Authentic isn't some ideal floating around in space until you magically find it, like an Easter egg or a New Age treasure hunt. True authenticity is only as good as what you do and who you love. Period. In that vein, I definitely made a mistake trusting Roger, but it won't be one I'll make again.

Bastard.

I look around. If nothing else, this place is aesthetically pleasing. All rolling hills and lush mountains and clear blue sky. I pick up a couple rocks and try skipping them in the fishing pond. They sink, which feels like an omen, and I decide I'd better get back inside before the cops show up and cosplay that I'm resisting arrest. It's still not lunchtime yet, though, so I return to the residence halls. Going to my room's as good an excuse as any—begging off that I was too tired to take that ridiculous test.

I type in the building code, essentially logging my whereabouts in a database somewhere and foregoing bodily autonomy. Once I'm buzzed in, I wander toward my room while fantasizing about what I'll tell Dr. Allegheny when he realizes I didn't finish the assessment.

I reach my room and push open the door. The first thing I register in my eyeline is movement. Then panic. Startled, I look up to see my roommate. Camila. I didn't think she'd be here, but the poor girl's dressed in this navy-blue bra top and shorts, and she's dancing in the center of our bedroom, her bare arms held high above her head. Or at least that's what she *was* doing.

She's now frozen mid-pose.

"Oh, sorry," I say. "Don't stop on my account."

"Get out!" she screams.

My eyes go wide. "What?"

"This is private!"

Retreat is not my natural instinct, but her voice is so shrill, so urgent, I immediately back out and pull the door shut behind me. My heart pounds with adrenaline. Holy hell. I'm not sure what just happened, but it wasn't good. Not at all.

I hesitate. Part of me wants to see if Camila's okay. She had *cuts* on her side. Bruises, too. But maybe I really did something wrong. Part of me bristles at being kicked out of my own space. I have just as much a right to it as she does. But I resist the indulgence of righteousness. I can't be mad at Camila. Not after what I saw in her eyes when she looked at me. That wasn't entitlement. It wasn't even rage.

It was the fear of exposure. Of being vulnerable.

And *that* I do understand.

TWENTY-THREE

CAMILA

DAMN IT.

I wipe tears from my cheeks, and God, this is all so pointless. She didn't see anything, I tell myself. Nothing bad, at least. She saw me *dancing*. That's it. It's nothing to be ashamed of, and in fact, it's what I *want* people to see me doing. That's kind of the whole point of performing. So why did I act like that?

What's wrong with me?

My hands shake as panic threatens to overwhelm me. It's like a predator closing in on its prey, eyes wild and maw gaping. It's also the earth opening up around me, a girl-size sinkhole yearning to pull me somewhere I can't escape. Brushing my hair back and steeling my shoulders, I do the only thing I know how to do—I start at the top.

And dance.

The music's all in my head; I don't have the space to spread out, but soon the movement calms me. This is the routine I performed for my audition. The one Ivan helped me choreograph.

The one that got me in.

By the time I'm done, I'm completely winded and sweat's pouring down my back. My fitness is shit. It's been almost a month since I was last in a real dance studio, and I reach to take a swig from my water bottle, the only one I'm allowed to keep in my room. The bottle's clear and it was assigned to me on intake and someone wrote my last name on it in Sharpie. Supposedly it's meant to keep us from guzzling booze or swallowing drain cleaner, but it certainly does nothing to keep me from wanting to.

This is when I remember Dani and how I acted, and I know I have to apologize. That's what you do when you freak out on someone for reasons that are impossible to explain and justify getting locked up in a psych ward. The thing is, I don't want to apologize, but this is the transactional thing I was trying to explain to Dr. Roberts. I just want to be able to be myself. But because I'm living with someone, I now have to smile and placate and consider how who I am affects a person I never asked to care about in the first place. It's beyond annoying.

It's insanity, actually.

But dutiful conformist that I am, I pull on a real shirt and jeans and slip out of the room in search of my roommate. It's nearly lunchtime, and it'd be best to catch her before she tells all the other girls what a bitch I am. I'm racing down the hallway to the stairs when I suddenly stop short. It's Dani. She's here. She's sitting on the top step, facing the first floor, picking at the skin around her fingernails.

"Hey," I say softly.

"Hey," she responds.

I need to do this now, I realize. Before I change my mind. "You're going to get an infection."

"What?" She turns to look at me.

I gesture toward her hands, then regret it because my own hands are shaking. "Your cuticles. They'll get infected if you keep playing with them like that. Mine always do."

"Ah."

"Can I talk to you for a minute?" I ask, forcing the words out fast and bracing for her response.

But Dani nods, and I settle on the steps beside her, trying to appear relaxed in a way that I really don't feel.

"I just wanted to say that I'm sorry. For, you know, freaking out on you back there."

She smiles. "You did freak out."

"I *know*."

"Well, apology accepted," she says.

I stare at her, confused. Is that it? Is that all she wants from me? "Well, uh, thanks."

Dani returns to her finger picking. "I'm sorry, too."

"What for?" I ask.

"I should've knocked before I came in. I'll do that from now on. I think only-childhood has spoiled me. It's kept me from learning some basic manners. Among other things."

"I'm an only child, too," I offer, leaning a little closer and letting our shoulders almost touch.

She smiles. "What's your family like?"

"Uptight."

"Tell me about it. Are they on you all the time about grades and clubs and college app shit?"

"No. They're not like that at all. They're more quiet, I guess? But my dad's pretty serious. He had a rough childhood—he's from Colombia originally, but he was adopted out of an orphanage when he was five and brought to the United States."

Dani's eyes go wide. "Why was he in an orphanage?"

"He doesn't remember."

"Nobody told him?"

I shake my head.

"Were the people who adopted him decent?"

"I guess. His adoptive dad died really young, though, and his mom was depressed a lot after that. It was hard on him. They were close, though."

"Were?"

"She died a few years back. Accidental overdose." I keep smiling. "What about you? What neuroses have your parents given you?"

Dani grumbles. "I don't think they've *given* me anything. They're just overbearing and hypocritical. Like, my mom only cares about image and if her picture's in the paper and if she's ahead in the polls for the next election."

"You said that earlier. What is she being elected for?"

"Reelected. She's on the city council in Dallas. You'd think she was running for governor, though, by how seriously she takes it."

"Maybe she will someday."

"God help us all," she mutters. Then: "You're not giving up on this dancing thing, huh? You looked kind of amazing based on what I saw."

"What do you mean giving up?" I ask.

"This school you got into. You still want to go?"

"More than anything."

We both jump and turn at the beep and creak of the building's main door opening down on the first floor. A beam of sunlight pours in. Followed by a voice calling out:

"Danielle Washington? Are you in here?"

TWENTY-FOUR

DANI

SAME AS IT EVER WAS.

When I finally get to meet the famous Christina Sánchez, it's because I'm in her office getting yelled at while she lectures me on the importance of rule following and "adherence to the treatment plan." It'd be infuriating if it weren't so tedious. But adults are all alike. Deep down they hate teenagers. They fear our power and our youth and the way it shines a light on their own failures, and so they all do their best to minimize and demean every aspect of our existence.

But I know better than to take it personally. Friend of my aunt or not, this woman isn't my mother, and after a couple of weeks here, I won't ever have to worry about seeing her again.

"Yeah, yeah, I get it," I tell her. "I should've told someone before I left the assessment thing."

"Is there a reason you didn't complete it?"

I shrug. "Didn't want to."

Dr. Sánchez gives a long sigh. "You know, we don't ask our clients to do busywork here. Completing that assessment is meant to be a crucial part of your treatment planning here at Peach Tree Hills. It allows us to identify a baseline of understanding for your relationship with substance use. It also helps us to contextualize your peer group and the messaging you've received regarding substance use."

"So it helps *you*," I say.

"That's right. And in helping us, we're better able to provide individualized treatment and interventions that are customized for your unique context."

"I never asked you to do that."

She ignores this. "Beyond the information gathering, it's disappointing to know that your response is not to ask for greater clarification regarding the relevance of certain activities but instead to just leave without communicating your thoughts."

"I didn't think that deeply about it," I say. "I just didn't want to fill out the test. That's all. It was three hundred multiple-choice questions. If you want to know something about me, you could always just ask."

Dr. Sánchez leans forward. "Danielle, I can appreciate that

the assessment is tedious and that perhaps the reason we wanted you to complete it was not made clear to you in a way that you could understand. I will speak with Dr. Allegheny and let him determine if there is an acceptable alternative to completing that measure."

I hold in a smirk. "That sounds great."

"But I'm going to need your agreement and understanding that participation here at Peach Tree Hills is a two-way street. Our staff can't help you if you aren't willing to help yourself. Is that clear?"

"Sure," I say because of course it's clear. Compliance has long been branded as "engagement"; free thinking as resistance.

Anyway, like I said:

Same as it ever was.

When I arrive late at my morning activity—"Joy in the Garden"— everyone's already hard at work. About a dozen or so girls are busy digging in the dirt with plastic hoes or else kneeling on these green padded mats while they pluck up weeds. Bees are buzzing everywhere, the sun's blazing, and while it's relatively quiet, there's not a lot of joy that I'm seeing, if you want to know the truth.

After grabbing a sun hat, I do my best to blend in. I'm not eager to be on everybody's shit list. Still, when a couple of the girls come over to ask why I was meeting with Dr. Sánchez and what I'd done to get in trouble, I don't hold my smirk back in the retelling.

A younger girl, Tess, with dark hair and pale skin, is more curious than the others. "So you got out of doing it? The standardized testing?"

"That's right."

She stabs her spade in the ground. "Good for you."

"Yeah, she said Dr. Allegheny would get the info he needs some other way. Which, I hope, involves just asking me and not some *Clockwork Orange*–style thought control measure."

Tess makes a *tsk-tsk* sound with her teeth. "It's all about thought insertion. And repetition. Everything they do here."

"Is that right?" I ask.

Her voice lowers. "You may have won this battle, but it'll be a Pyrrhic victory. You'll pay. They'll make sure of that."

"How will they make me pay?"

The girl resumes hacking at the ground. With each motion, her bangs flop across her forehead. "I don't know yet. But that's the nature of the mental health industrial complex. They need us to be sick in order to have any power. You realize that, don't you? Nothing is as it seems."

"Yeah, sure." I falter a bit and turn my attention to the planting bed in front of me.

But Tess creeps closer, still swinging that blade around. Plastic or not, it's a little unsettling. "The only thing wrong with any of us is that we've all questioned the protocol at some point in our lives. That's why we're here. We're not the sick ones. It's the people running everything who are sick. None of us were born for what the world has in store for us—endless toiling followed by consumption. We were created to be cogs in the giant assembly line of capitalism and imperialism, where free will no longer exists. Our happiness, our lives, are only valued for how willing we are to keep the whole game going."

"Watch it!" I shove my own tool in the path of her own to keep her from chopping my foot off.

"Sorry," she says in a way that suggests she isn't.

"You've really thought a lot about this, haven't you?" I ask. "All our toiling and joyless consumption."

Tess squints, wary. "Are you making fun of me?"

"I'm really not."

"Well, you'd better not be."

"I said I *wasn't*."

The expression on the girl's face tells me she thinks I'm full of shit, but I'm not interested in continuing this conversation any more than she is. Once she drifts away, I return to my task, which is tilling the soil for sunflowers. Seems kind of pointless, if you ask me. I guess the seeds taste good, but as a production crop, the size-to-bounty ratio feels minimal.

Yolanda, who's supposedly leading this enriching activity, sidles over to me. She's wearing a huge sun hat and a fresh pair of khakis this morning, which is bold, considering how dirty we're all getting thanks to Tess's over-vigorous digging.

"How's it going?" she chirps.

"Pretty hot out here," I answer.

"You should see it in the summer."

"Don't think I'll be here for that."

She wipes her brow, pulls at the brim of her hat, and squints at me. "I see."

"So are these just activities to pass the time? Or is there some deeper meaning I'm missing?"

"What do you think?" she asks.

I shrug. "The gardening part feels like indentured servitude, but it's producing food, so that's a real purpose. Don't know about the rest. But if you're writing grants or books or giving lectures or otherwise making money off what you make us do in here, then I guess there's some hustle in it that I can admire. Even if I'm the one who's being exploited."

Yolanda offers the faintest of smiles. "I appreciate your encouragement, Dani. And I'll keep checking in with you about how you feel during our various activities, if that's all right?"

"Fine by me."

"Excellent!" she says.

TWENTY-FIVE

CAMILA

THE BEST THING that happens all day is discovering that lunch isn't some big group activity where we all have to sit down together and say grace and eat at the same time. Instead, there's a forty-minute time period where we can grab a meal from the kitchen and eat in either the main dining room or out on the picnic tables.

I opt for staying inside, since that's where the fewest people are. A nurse brings my medication over and watches me swallow. When she's gone, I open the brown paper bag with my name on it and find a turkey wrap, an apple, and a small packet of almonds. My appetite's still nonexistent, but I force a few bites down.

"How is it?" a girl asks, and I don't think I recognize her. She's freckled and thin, and her skin's so pale it feels as if I can see through to her veins.

"Not bad," I say.

"Can I sit with you?"

"Of course." It's not my place to tell her no, although there's nothing I loathe more than eating with other people. Well, it's the expectation of it that gets to me. And from what I've observed, it's like an obsession, the way certain people insist that everyone in a specified group has to be on the same schedule and eat the same food and generally perform these creepy mealtime rituals in the name of some false intimacy idol.

But eating isn't social. How could it be when you're just stuffing food into your mouth before turning it into shit? Anyway, it's one of those obligations I really resent, and I'm just glad my own parents aren't into forced family dining. It's like we all get how pointless it is. You can feel close to a person and still not want to watch them eat egg salad or be forced to explain your own dietary choices.

"What's your name?" I ask the girl.

"It's Mel," she says shyly. "Short for Melissa. You're Camila, right? You arrived yesterday?"

I nod. "How about you? When did you get here?"

"It's been a while," she says. "I've kind of lost track."

"You've lost track?"

"What're you here for?" Mel asks.

I shrug. "Doing something stupid."

"Aren't we all."

"Why? What'd you do?" I say.

She pushes her food around. "I don't think I want to talk about it any more than you do."

"Okay." This feels confusing, since she had to know I'd ask about her if she asked about me first. That's the social contract. We all follow it. Or so I thought.

"I shouldn't have asked you in the first place," Mel mumbles.

"It's fine," I tell her, but warning bells are going off in my head. I don't like where this conversation is going.

"I'm really sorry." Mel stares down at her lunch, and now I'm horrified to see tears welling up in her eyes.

"Uh, do you know if the computer room is open?" I ask quickly.

"Should be." She sniffles. "But you'd better hurry."

"Why?"

"It's lunch now. But in twenty minutes, it'll be a classroom for the students who are doing online school."

"Who has to do that?"

She lifts her head to show me her watery face. "Almost everyone has to at some point. Your doctor will tell you when they think you're ready."

"Great." I gather up my trash and prepare to leave the table. "Hey, thanks for the info."

"That's what I'm here for," Mel says sadly.

I can't help myself. Once online again, I pull up the email from Fieldbrook and just stare at it. They want me. They really do. They believe in me.

And I can't go.

The fingers of my left hand slip beneath my shirt to press the wounds that live there, although they're mostly scabbed over. I poke harder, but honestly, reading this email feels more like self-harm than anything I can do with a dippy pair of travel tweezers. But maybe Dani was right. Maybe I'm not giving up on going yet.

But how?

A surge of energy comes over me. I've always been good at problem-solving when the problem doesn't involve emotional relationships with other people. And my therapist seemed to say that people don't show up for you just on account of transactional reasons, and so maybe I can learn to make an emotional appeal.

Maybe it just takes practice.

Both hands back on the keyboard, I engage in some hasty research, seeking out possible funding sources that I can reach out to. Supporters of the arts. Professional dance companies. Anyone. There are only two weeks left until I have to inform Fieldbrook of my decision, so I don't have time to be picky. Or to second-guess my choices.

After ten feverish minutes, I acquire contact info for a dozen separate organizations. It's not a lot, but it's a start. I've also drafted a template email. It's rough, but reads:

> To Whom It May Concern,
>
> I am writing to you because I am a student in Georgia who is seeking to further my education and experience in dance by attending the prestigious Fieldbrook Academy in New Jersey. I have already been accepted based on my audition, but unfortunately, my family does not have the financial resources to allow me to attend. This is why I am reaching out to you at this time. I understand that you very generously offer scholarships to students who display great promise in the performing arts. Although I will not be attending college next year, it is my dream to major in dance at one of the best schools in the country. In order to do that, being able to attend Fieldbrook Academy is essential. I would be extremely grateful if you would consider me for one of your scholarships, and of course, I'm happy to repay generosity in any way that you ask. I have a 3.7 GPA, and with regard

to dance, I am eager to study contemporary, modern, jazz, and ballroom.

Thank you for your consideration.

Sincerely,

Camila Ortiz

It's not great, but the best I can hope for is that the message conveys the sincerity and humility I genuinely feel. After looking over my shoulder, I quickly send out the emails, and in a last impulsive move, I send one to Ivan and his parents. It's not that they're super rich or their studio is that successful. It's in Lamont, after all. But any amount helps, and after reading Ivan's message to me, it feels right. By Dr. Roberts's standards, he's the closest thing I have to a real friend.

Isn't that what they're for?

Slipping back out with mere minutes to spare, I hurry to my next scheduled therapy meeting. It's a group thing, and when I get to the assigned room, everyone's seated in a circle on brightly colored floor pillows.

"Sit anywhere," says this nerdy-looking guy with glasses and a bad haircut that's straight out of 2004. He's also seated on a floor pillow with his spine straight, and he's got his legs crossed in such a way that one of his shoes rests gently atop the opposite knee. I'm impressed. Nerdy or not, that takes flexibility.

Spotting Dani on the far side of the room, I make a beeline for the floor pillow next to hers. Once seated, I promptly pull my own legs into the same pose as the man's. He clocks the effort and offers a nod in acknowledgment.

"We'll begin in about five minutes." He holds his hand up, showing off all five fingers. "My name's Charles, by the way."

I turn to Dani. "Hey, what happened with you earlier? Is everything okay?"

"It was fine," she says after a moment.

"Really?" Her tone doesn't sound like it was fine.

"Yeah, but this place is full of shit. Some crazy conspiracy-theory girl tried to convert me earlier."

"Conspiracy theory?"

Dani waves a hand. "She was going on about some Illuminati or Q-type stuff that had to do with mind control and being enslaved by the deep state or whatever."

"Maybe she's got some paranoia thing going on. I kind of know what that's like," I say slowly. "Or maybe she has her reasons for believing what she does. Either way, I don't think labels are a helpful way of talking about her."

But Dani sulks. "Maybe she's a *bitch*. I want to get out of here, though. I don't like this place. This isn't what I thought it would be."

"Can you do that? Can you just leave?"

Her eyes flash. "They can't keep me. Not against my will."

I bite my lip but don't say anything, since (1) Dani seems upset, and (2) I happen to know from experience that there are absolutely times when you can be kept somewhere against your will. But I also know that not having money is often the line between what passes for freedom these days or feeling like your life is being controlled by the deep state, aka late-stage capitalism. So, you know, maybe the girl Dani talked to isn't crazy after all.

Maybe she's just stuck.

Like the rest of us.

TWENTY-SIX

DANI

"I HATE IT HERE," I tell Dr. Allegheny the next time I see him. "I probably hate you, too."

"How's that?" he asks.

"You got me in trouble the other day."

"*That's* why you hate it here?"

"It's why I hate you."

"I see."

I pull on a thread on the end of my shirt. "I think I'm really getting sick. Worse than ever. Or maybe I'm going crazy."

"Why do you say that?"

"I thought I had a fever last night. The night before, too. I woke up all covered in sweat. And when I eat, I want to puke. But that might be the food. It seriously sucks. I hope you bring your own lunch. For your sake."

Dr. Allegheny folds his hands together. Oh, and the yellow Crocs are back, by the way. "It sounds like you're having a hard time of it."

"I really hate it here."

"You said that."

I sink farther in my chair and push my shoes across the carpet. "I can't believe places like this exist. That you're just allowed to lock kids up when their parents don't want to deal with them anymore. Shouldn't that be illegal? What about human rights?"

"You feel like your parents don't want to deal with you?"

"They basically told me as much. Well, that's not how they framed it. But how they framed it was even worse."

"How so?"

I sit up. Fan myself. "Do you have any water? It's fucking hot in here."

Dr. Allegheny brings me a Dixie cup of tap water, which I kind of want to complain about, but I'm too thirsty to protest. I guzzle it down and ask for another. He obliges but then settles back in his leather club chair without asking if I need anything else.

"You don't seem very worried about me," I tell him.

"What should I be worried about?"

"You're a doctor. You can't tell that I'm sick?"

"I *am* a doctor. Which is why we're seeing each other. Because you're sick."

I flip him off.

Dr. Allegheny cocks his head. "Have you wondered if part of the reason you feel so bad lately is that you're depressed?"

"I'm definitely not depressed."

"Or maybe it's because you're sober."

I glare. "This again?"

"You know, in drug addiction treatment, we talk about two kinds of dependence—physical and psychological. Physical dependence is what leads to withdrawal symptoms. Heroin or opioids are what people usually think of, but from a medical standpoint, one of the most dangerous substances to withdraw from is alcohol. For people who have been drinking heavily for years, it can be deadly to stop cold turkey."

"Fucking great," I say.

"But there's also psychological dependence. Because taking a substance to feel good is not necessarily a terrible thing. But for people who don't feel good during other times in their life, there can be a risk of becoming dependent on the drug to control one's emotions, which makes it that much harder to stop. Because now you have to find a new way of dealing with bad or uncomfortable emotions, which are what the drugs have helped you avoid all this time."

"You're saying the reason I feel so crappy right now is

because this is just how I normally feel and I have to find a new way to deal with that?"

Dr. Allegheny considers this. "In a way, yes. I guess that is what I'm saying."

"Jesus," I breathe. "That whole thing you just said, it's so goddamn infuriating. I really, really hate it."

To my surprise, he laughs.

"What?" I ask. "What's so funny?"

"You're not wrong," he says.

After therapy, I head back to the residence hall. The Georgia heat's coming on strong, and I'm dying to change out of these pants. It's weird, though. After that back-and-forth with Dr. Allegheny, my headache's faded. It's been replaced by a funny buzzing inside my chest, like a nest of hummingbirds are flapping around in there, ready to break free.

Skipping up the flight of stairs and approaching my room, I'm careful to knock this time. When Camila's muffled "Come in" floats through the door, I march in, my mood bigger, brighter than it's been for days.

"Hey there," I say.

Only Camila doesn't look at me. She's seated at her desk with a nubby golf pencil in hand and a pile of scrap paper heaped around her. I watch as she scribbles furiously, and honestly, I don't think she's supposed to have a pencil or anything sharp, so I don't know where that came from.

"Working on something?" I ask.

Her head bobs. "Uh-huh."

"Need help?"

She whirls around, her eyes wide but wary. Her hair's down, dark curls spilling over her bare shoulders, and the girl's *gorgeous*, I realize. It's not something you notice at first—she's too quiet and sullen—but even though her body's sort of tight, all dancer perfect, what's most striking about Camila is her intensity. It's electric.

"Can you write?" she asks.

"Yes," I say. "Did you think I couldn't?"

She pulls her hair to one side. "No, I mean, are you *good* at writing? Like, business letters. That's what I'm trying to do, but I don't have a lot of experience with people in authority and asking them for things."

"Asking for what?" I walk over to the bolted-down dresser and pull open my drawer to rummage around for my yellow-and-black sundress. "I'm listening, by the way."

"Money," she says.

I slip out of my earlier clothes and pull on the dress, shimmying into its tight top. "You're writing fundraiser letters? Like for a charity? Yeah, I am good at that. My mom does a lot of development work and grant writing. Mostly for her own campaign, obviously. But I definitely know the language and tone."

"You do?"

"Who are you raising money for?" I ask.

"Me," she says, and when she sees my puzzled expression: "That dance school I told you about? The one I applied to without telling my parents? I mean, it's a long shot, I know, but I still want to go. I have to. I've worked so hard for this, and it's just a matter of finding the money."

"Doesn't the school have financial aid? They should be able to help you out."

"It's not enough. I filled out the financial aid forms using the amounts from the prior years. My parents don't make a lot. My dad works for the city, and my mom's a dental hygienist. Anyway, I included the savings I thought they had and now they don't and now we can't pay. Or that's what they told me, at least."

"What do you mean?" I ask.

She shrugs. "Well, you said it. They're able to afford to send me here, right? It's not cheap."

"You think they're lying to you? About not having the money?"

"I don't know. But the school denied my aid appeal."

"How much do you need?" I ask. "For your tuition?"

Camila blushes. "Twenty thousand dollars. Per year. So forty total."

I whistle. "That's a lot of money."

"I know." Her blush grows deeper. "But now I think I can do something. I can contact people who give out scholarships and plead my case. Don't you think that might help? I sent out a few emails today, but I want to send out more. Anywhere that might be able to help."

I hesitate. "How much time do you have to figure this out?"

"Two weeks. Until May thirtieth."

"That's soon," I say.

"I *know*."

"Okay."

"So can you help me?"

"I can try," I offer. "My mom knows people who support the arts back home in Texas. She does, too, but usually through the foundation she works with. They have grants and such, although I know there's an application season and a whole process. It's . . ." I pause. It's clear Camila is hanging on to my every word and also that I'm talking about a whole world she knows nothing about.

"Yes," I say. "I can help. Let me look at what you've got."

Camila lets out this big sigh and shoves her notebook at me, where's she's written a draft of a letter. I wince at some of the language she's using: *I'm happy to repay your generosity in any way that you ask . . .*

"What?" she says.

I take the pencil from her and start to cross out some of

her lines, adding in my own. "It's nothing. It's just, you sound like you're offering more than what you really are. Almost like a sugar baby or something. But we can punch this up and really package you as someone they're going to want to support. It's not about your gratitude or how nice you are or any favors you have to offer. It's about selling yourself as someone who'll make them look good for supporting you. That's how you talk to donors. There's a whole language to it, but in the end, they just want a little prestige with their charity."

"What's a sugar baby?" Camila asks.

"You know. It's someone who's seeking certain arrangements. Money in exchange for . . ."

Her eyes widen. "That's not the impression I want to give."

"Didn't think so." I scoot back and pluck a fresh piece of paper from the desk. "Okay, before we get started, I want to ask you some questions. That'll help me figure out how to frame your future career."

"Seriously?"

"You ready?"

"As I'll ever be," Camila says.

"Let's do this."

TWENTY-SEVEN

CAMILA

IT'S BEEN TWO DAYS since Dani started helping me with finding scholarship money or a grant for my tuition, and already I feel different. Not good, exactly. Just different. More awake. More alive, even.

"Maybe it's the medication," my shrink tells me.

"Maybe."

"How're you sleeping?"

"Really well. My dreams are wild. I don't remember the last time I had dreams this vivid."

"And your anxiety?"

"Ever present."

"Is the Xanax helping?"

"I think so. It's hard to say."

She nods. "I want you to stay on it for now, okay? We can reevaluate in a couple of weeks. Your recovery is really just starting."

"How long will it take?"

"Recovery? That depends."

"On what?" I hate these kinds of answers. *They're* what give me anxiety.

"That's a good question." Dr. Roberts sets her notepad down. "I'd say a large part of your recovery depends on us figuring out what led to your suicide attempt in the first place."

"Seems kind of obvious," I tell her.

"It's not obvious to me. I think there's the attempt itself and the circumstances surrounding that event. But there are also all the things in your life that contributed to you feeling as if ending your life was the only way you could find relief from the pain you were experiencing. I know we've talked about the disappointment of not being able to go to the dance academy, but I've gotten the sense during our time together—as well as your history of self-harm—that a lot of that pain you've been feeling has been with you for a long time. For years, actually."

"So what causes it? The pain?"

She nods. "That's what we're going to try and figure out."

"Are you saying we haven't started yet?"

"Well, when a patient's in crisis, the immediate focus has

to be on safety and stabilization. In addition to the day treatment program you attended, you'll notice that right from the start we've incorporated treatment interventions such as medication, sleep hygiene, good nutrition, structured activity, movement, connection to nature, and social support. These are aimed at promoting physical well-being, which is crucial for the treatment of depression and anxiety."

"You still haven't said what's wrong with me."

"I said we're still figuring that out. Once we do, we'll have a clearer picture of your recovery path. And of course, you'll have input, too."

"How?"

"By creating your own goals and increments of progress. As your therapist, your safety is my top priority. That's why we do our ongoing assessment of any suicidal ideation and self-harming behaviors. But I consider my role as primarily helping my clients clarify their personal values and assisting them in integrating these values more fully in their own lives."

"Values?" I echo.

"That's right."

"How do I know what mine are?"

"That's something we can work on together. We can even start right now. How does that sound?"

"Whatever," I say. "Yeah, it's fine."

Later, I find myself with a whole hour free before dinner. And I know what I *should* be doing with this time, and it's definitely not journaling about what I think makes a Morally Good Person like Dr. R told me to do. But to do that, I'd have to write about honesty, and I wasn't totally honest with her. Not today. Not ever.

She'd flip if she knew about the tweezers hidden in my mattress, which is why I don't tell her. In that way, they're a secret for me and me alone, and I don't know—secrets feel good sometimes. Keeping them, that is. But also, it's not like having them's going to kill me, and I am honest about my *feelings*. How I think about death a lot but not about doing it. Just the fact that I *could*. If I had to. Although I'm also thinking about other things. Like how I need to get to the library and look up additional places to send out the fundraising letters Dani's been helping me with.

She also told me to make a GoFundMe account and a Patreon, but they both sound miserable. Humiliating, really. I remember attending a dance competition where one of the teams had to fundraise for their outfits, and even though it was supposed to be this amazing uplifting story of perseverance, I just hated it. The whole idea. Hell, I'd rather be a sugar baby. There's more dignity in that—an honest and transparent exchange of services and money, freed from the notion of charity. Or worse, pity. Besides,

I sincerely doubt I'll be able to access any fundraising sites on the Peach Tree Hills computers.

I'm almost at the library door. As I peer over my shoulder to make sure no one's looking, I happen to catch sight of a different building. It's the yoga studio, which is set back from the courtyard, closer to the meadow. Everything about it is inviting. The small building's framed by pots of bamboo, and the roof has one of those living gardens on top of it. Also, the sliding glass door appears to be open, and before I know it, I'm walking toward it, then cautiously peering in.

The studio's empty, and staring into it feels like staring at a desert mirage. It's just too perfect. The glossy wood floor. The mirrored wall.

And me.

Before I know it, I'm stepping inside. I'm sliding off my shoes, my shirt, and stripping down to the sports bra beneath. Something I never do unless I'm alone. Completely alone. Otherwise, I always perform in leotards, anything that covers my torso. But now I spin around, slowly at first, taking in the space—its shape and corners. Every stage has its own personality, and every dancer knows to take their time getting acquainted with that most formative partner. When I'm ready, when I've breathed in all I can of the acoustics, the dimensions, the world beneath me, I begin to stretch out. My first movements are exploration. Stretching. Bending. Testing.

It's been a while, my muscles tell me as they surge and reach beyond what the cramped boundaries of my tiny dorm room have to offer.

Where have you been?

The answer comes quickly. I test more, and soon I feel it in the ache of my arches, the niggling burn in my lumbar region, and in the hollow space carved by my kicks that don't reach as high as I know they're capable of.

Where have *I* been?

And this is when my body truly responds. I don't need music. The beat, the melody, I carry them with me. Now my pulse rises in sync with my movement. My intention. I leap gently, focusing on technique and not power. The landing feels good; the floor springing back to push me into the air again.

And again.

Here I am, I think.

I'm right here.

Still.

TWENTY-EIGHT

DANI

I WAKE UP Thursday morning with a tingle of anticipation brewing in my gut.

"What time is she coming?" Camila asks from across the room.

"Eight sharp," I say, and the she in question is my aunt Bea, who is stopping by this morning. She even gets to have breakfast with me.

"That's nice." Camila yawns and pulls the blankets over her head while I gather up my belongings for a shower.

Once I'm done and clean, I wrap the thin terry-cloth towel around my body and rub cheap institutional lotion over my leg stubble. No razors allowed, but I'll be damned if I'm going to walk around with ashy calves and ankles.

Other girls start streaming in. Breakfast is at eight, and everyone basically rolls out of bed and heads to the dining room at the same time. A couple of the girls wave at me and smile, but one looks quizzically at my shower cap.

"How often do you wash it?" she asks.

"As often as you wash your ass," I tell her.

The girl laughs. Back in my room, I drop the towel and pull on my favorite clothes—a vertical-striped dress that flares at the hips but also has pockets, and a pair of white Converse. Mornings are chilly, so at the last moment, I grab a hunter-green denim jacket and wriggle into the sleeves.

Camila's still asleep.

"You need to get up," I tell her.

She groans. "What time is it?"

"Seven fifty. I'm heading out now. My aunt should be here any minute."

"Five more minutes," she says.

"Okay." I run gloss over my lips, put on deodorant—almost forgot—and leave.

It's brisk out, before the sun's had a chance to get going for the day. The lawn's still covered in night dew, and the flowers are shut tight. There's even mist rising off the pond, and a bunch of birds are huddling around a feeder near the willow tree. Walking to the main building, those tingles of nerves return to my stomach. It's not worry or anything. More . . . uncertainty. I don't know why my aunt's coming today. I just got a note last night that she was coming and that we would be having breakfast. Maybe it's just that. A social call.

Or maybe it's something else.

My hope is that we're going to talk about an exit strategy. More specifically an exit strategy that involves my moving in with her. I've been here ten days now, which is close to my two-week commitment, and I haven't been kicked out or arrested or even done anything illicit. Total good behavior.

If you ask me, this alone should earn me a year in Atlanta, finishing up high school. I'd be cool about the whole thing. I really would. I'm not looking to party or raise hell. I just want to be treated like an adult and trusted to make adult choices. Like, it's not a big deal to smoke a little weed or get a little loose with some close friends. You know? It's what people do. It's how you make connections. I kind of can't wait.

Well, the note I got told me to meet my aunt at good old Dr. Sánchez's office, and upon entering the front door and going to reception, I'm quickly waved back. The door's half-open, but I knock first—I know my manners—before peeking my head in.

"Dani!"

"Aunt Bea!" I squeal, running across the room to hug her as my earlier wariness fades. This is my life, I remind myself, buried in her arms and inhaling the sweet scent of her perfume. This is who I am.

Dr. Sánchez stands, watching us, until we break apart. "Dani, I told your aunt that you two could have breakfast in here. Someone should be bringing it in shortly, and I will let you two visit for now."

"Thanks, C," my aunt says, and I wave as Dr. Sánchez departs. Then the two of us are able to settle on the small love seat by the window.

"I'm so glad you're here," I tell her, and it's funny, seeing my aunt all dressed up in business clothes. She must have work later, so that makes sense, but it adds to the surrealness of the moment.

"I'm glad, too." She squeezes my hand, smiles. "Tell me what you've been up to."

"Oh, you know. Just doing what they tell me to."

"Such as?"

"I go to therapy. Do art. It's all very wholesome. Oh, also my psychiatrist is Black."

"Who is it?" she asks. Then: "No, don't tell me. It's possible I could know him, and I don't want to influence anything."

"You won't influence anything. He's fine, I guess. Oh, and they make me work in the garden. Nothing like a little forced labor in the South."

"Dani." Aunt Bea frowns. "I thought you were going to take this seriously."

"I *am*."

Yolanda walks in, carrying two covered trays that she sets on the coffee table in front of us. My aunt thanks her, and I'm reminded of all the times I ordered room service while staying in hotels with my mom when we would travel the state for volleyball competitions. I was competitive through junior high until I got bored.

"How's the food?" my aunt asks.

I pull the lid from both of our trays to reveal steaming plates of scrambled eggs, grilled tomatoes, and wheat toast. "It's okay. It's not Texas, though."

"Not enough steak for you?"

"Not enough flavor."

Aunt Bea laughs and takes a bite of her toast.

"So why are you here?" I ask.

"I kind of pushed Christina on it a little. I'm not sure it's totally within the rules, but she said it would be fine given the circumstances of how you ended up here."

"What does that mean?"

"Just, well, that I felt a little weird about it. Calling your parents up and trying to convince them to sign off on their kid going to some facility they know nothing about."

"Come on," I say. "I bet Mom had a full background check run on every employee here before she agreed."

"She probably did." She puts the toast down. "But I feel responsible, so I wanted to come here and make sure you were okay. To know that this is really the right place for you and that you're getting the help you need."

My eyes narrow. "Did she tell you do this? To come check on me?"

"I offered."

"Aunt Bea . . ."

"I said I feel responsible," she insists. "I care about you, but I'm not a parent. I don't know that it was the right thing to do. I probably should've sent you back to Texas. I don't blame my sister for being a little . . . peeved."

"But you know what she's like. It's always a game with her. Everything is. She's just punishing you for making a choice without her."

"Maybe . . ." she says.

"Aunt Bea, you told me what she was like when you two were growing up. She's so focused on how other people see her that she doesn't care about hurting the people who are closest to her. It's evil."

"It's not evil. She's just . . . misguided. But I understand how it can feel that way."

I feel a knot of dread in my chest. "She did send you, didn't she?"

"It's not a big deal. I wanted to come."

"So what's her problem with this place?" I ask. "Is she worried she won't get all the glory for my miraculous recovery? Or is it not 'faith-based' enough for bragging rights? Is it too *permissive* with its holistic model of treatment? I bet she called it a 'summer camp.' She did, didn't she?"

My aunt sighs. "She just wants to know how it's going. And your parents, ultimately, are the ones who get to determine whether you stay or not. So it would behoove you—and me— if you could help me report back that everything is going well and that you are getting with the program and doing what she wants."

"It's always about what she wants!" I wail. "This is supposed to be about me. For once!"

I snap my jaw shut at the sound of my own echoing pitifulness. What's wrong with me? Why am I arguing for what I don't need?

Because maybe I do, I realize. Maybe I need this. But I'm not allowed to. Not on my terms, anyway.

"I know this is about you," my aunt says. "You think I don't know that?"

"*She* doesn't." I sulk. "And if she's not satisfied with your report, then what?"

"That's up to her."

"She wants you to fail, too. You know that, don't you?"

"That doesn't matter."

But it does. That's just it. Everything matters. It's all some sort of scorecard with her, and I'm not allowed to win. I came into this meeting ready to beg my aunt to let me leave and go home with her and get on with my life. But now I can't let that happen. I won't let her beat me.

"Fine," I say stiffly. "What does she need to hear?"

My aunt's expression turns apologetic. "You know."

I sigh and blink back tears. Then I take a deep breath and steady myself. "I'm working hard on my substance abuse problem. I've been sober from all drugs for the past ten days, and the only thing I'm allowed to take is Tylenol when I get a headache. I go to therapy every day—sometimes more than once a day—and I'm learning new coping skills that are constructive and not self-destructive. I am trying to be a better person. I'm trying to be a better daughter, too."

And so there it is. I've taken power back from my mother by testifying to the success of the program she didn't choose. But that's not all I have to do to declare victory.

I also have to fail.

TWENTY-NINE

CAMILA

"CAMILA," A VOICE SAYS. "Camila, wake up."

My eyes open, and I sit up straight. Look around. And it's the weirdest thing, but one of the nurses is in my room.

"What's happening?" I ask.

"You overslept."

"But I saw you earlier. You brought my medication."

She purses her lips. "Apparently you fell back asleep instead of getting up."

I yawn. "Dani said I still had ten minutes."

"Dani's not here."

"She's not?"

"It's almost nine, Camila."

My eyes widen. "Oh, crap. I'm sorry. I'm really sorry."

"It's vital that you stick to the schedule."

"I know."

"Then I'll let you get dressed, and in five minutes, I'll walk with you to your doctor's appointment."

"What doctor?" I ask. "I have group now."

"Dr. Roberts requested to see you this morning."

"Why? I don't think we're supposed to meet."

"Five minutes," she says. "Hurry up."

Once she's gone, I figure out the whole clothing thing, but I don't get why it's so urgent. I missed breakfast. So what? It's not a big deal, except I guess it is, and now I have to see Dr. Roberts and listen to her tell me why I've been so irresponsible or how my laziness doesn't align with my values of having a good work ethic or whatever.

Honestly, I should just go back to bed.

I don't, though, because I said I wouldn't and that's the suckiest thing of all. I pull on a pair of jeans, yesterday's T-shirt, and sandals. My thighs and calves ache as I move, but in a good way. A way that reminds me of secrets that are mine and mine alone. I pull my hair back in lieu of brushing it, then step out of the room.

The nurse is waiting, just like I knew she would be.

"Ready?" she says.

"As I'll ever be."

I can tell something bad's happened the moment I step into Dr. Roberts's office. It's hard to say exactly why. Maybe it's her body language—the tension in her shoulders; the way she's hunched forward in her chair as if she wants to get up and leave the room, anything so that she doesn't have to have this conversation with me.

Whatever it is, I *know*.

"What is it?" I ask. "I said I was sorry for oversleeping. I didn't think it was such a big deal."

Dr. Roberts blinks, then recovers. "No, that's not it, Camila. That's not a problem. I just needed to speak with you about something. That's why I asked to see you this morning."

"What did you want to talk about?"

"Why don't you sit down."

"You're scaring me," I say. "Did something happen to my parents?"

She shakes her head. "That's not it. No. Everyone's fine. Please don't worry."

"Okay."

She rolls her chair toward me once I'm seated. "But I did hear from your parents last night. Well, our director did and she contacted me, and that's why I wanted to speak with you. Your parents got in touch because they'd heard from your dance studio that you'd been emailing them and asking for financial support to help you attend the academy you were accepted into."

My heart crumples when I hear this. Or maybe it's more like collapsing or imploding, but whatever the word, it's an act of destruction. Of being destroyed. Because even as I feel myself falling forward, falling away, I'm still watching her lips move, I'm still hearing her words, but before she even says it, my mind puts it together. Her posture, her tension, her fears. She knows, and so now I know exactly what she's going to say and how deeply it will devastate me.

Before she even says it.

THIRTY

DANI

SOMETHING'S GOING ON with Camila. And by that, I mean I can't find her anywhere. She doesn't show up at group that morning. Or to lunch. She's also not in our room when I stop by after lunch, and honestly, she could've been abducted by aliens for all I know. It's mostly annoying because I can't bitch to her about the shit my mom's trying to pull and how she's able to exert her control over me all the way from Dallas.

The plot surrounding Camila's absence thickens during afternoon ecotherapy when I ask Yolanda what the hell is going on and she tells me to focus on my own responsibilities and personal growth.

"I thought learning to care about other people *was* one of

my personal responsibilities," I snap from where I'm crouched on the ground, plucking weeds from around a muddy patch of tomato seedlings. "Sounds like maybe I should focus all my energy into being a self-centered narcissist with no capacity for empathy or insight."

"No one's told you to do anything like that," Yolanda says with a sigh. "But maybe consider how spending all your time fighting authority or trying to goad people into submission is also a way that you avoid focusing on your own life."

I snort. "You sound like one of those posters you get at the book fair. The ones with the kittens?"

"You're still not focusing on yourself," she says.

"Can I have some juice?" I ask. "It's hot out here."

"That's all we've got until break." She points to a stack of Dixie cups and the sweaty orange water jug that sits perched on top of the split-rail fence.

I squint up at her. "This place is just one big disappointment after the other. You know that, right?"

She cups her ear. "I didn't hear an 'I' statement in there."

"Is she okay?" I ask. "Can't you even tell me that?"

"I don't know anything," Yolanda says in a low voice. "But I haven't heard otherwise, and you know, confidentiality is a real thing around here."

"I *know*." I go back to my weeding. "Thanks or whatever."

My mood remains foul up through break, although we have a respite from the usual fruit-and-cheese offerings. Instead, outside on the patio, a group of girls are serving ice cream.

"It's homemade," they announce proudly, and for the first time, I realize that there's a whole group separate from our gardening one, who work in the kitchen and help prepare the meals. I wonder how they decide which one to put us in—and if there are others that I'm not aware of. Anyway, it's kind of a heartwarming thing, which I know sounds super sappy. But I don't know. I guess I like the sense that despite all my complaining, we really are working toward a common goal. Makes me less resentful of the whole system, I guess. At least a little bit.

"What flavor?" I ask the girl who's scooping.

"Strawberry," she says. "Nothing's ripe yet, but there were some canned fruits we still had from last season that hadn't been used."

"Were you here then?" I ask.

She nods as she hands me a dish and spoon.

I'm incredulous. "You've been here a full year? Seriously?"

"No," she says. "But I was here then."

"And?"

She meets my gaze. "And now I'm back."

"Oh." I thank the girl and turn to go, and that's when I

finally see Camila. She's walking toward the dining patio, and I'm so relieved that I bound right over to her. Shove the ice cream in her face.

"Want some?"

"No, thanks," she says.

"Where've you been?" I ask. "I haven't seen you all day."

She shrugs. "Nowhere special. Just meetings. I guess."

I peer at her closely. Camila's not a super-outgoing person, but something about her is off. Her eyes are glassy. Unfocused.

"You look high," I tell her.

Her lips flick into a smile. "I wish."

"Really?"

"Kind of. What's this?" She nods at the crowded table of girls.

"They're the ones who made the ice cream."

"Ah." She stares at them for a while.

"You okay?" I ask.

"Yeah." Camila turns back to me. "Hey, you want to do something with me?"

"Like what?" I ask.

"Come on. I'll show you." She reaches for my hand and surprises me by pulling me with her. I didn't think she had it in her, the sheer will to lead.

Even more surprising: I follow.

THIRTY-ONE

CAMILA

"WHERE ARE WE GOING?" Dani asks, but I keep marching until we're out of sight from the other girls and the ice cream and all that laughter and noise. We duck behind the admin building and head into the trees. The whole time, I keep waiting for someone to run after us or call our names, but no one does.

"I just needed to breathe," I say when we're finally in the shade and alone. Up ahead I spot the neighboring fence line. It's a stone fence, and a trickling stream runs alongside it. Frogs are croaking, and I watch as a mosquito lands on my arm. Takes a bite.

"Are you sure you're okay?" Dani asks.

"Did I say I was okay?"

She frowns. "Yes. You did."

I stop walking and turn to look at her. "My parents called."

"You talked to them?"

"No. They talked to my shrink."

"About what?"

My chest hurts. "Forget it. I just— It's just hard sometimes."

"Being here?" she asks.

"Being anywhere."

Dani pops the last of her ice cream in her mouth and gives a furtive glance over her shoulder. "Were you thinking about leaving? Is that why you came out here?"

I look at the stone fence. It would be easy to step over. It would be easy to go.

"Let's do it," I say without really thinking, and Dani doesn't argue. We both hop over, and that's that. No security guard comes running, and no alarms go off, which is weird, when you think about it. We were there, and now we're here.

We're free.

Is this really happening?

In what feels like a dream, I start off in the lead, pushing through thick undergrowth and brush—there's no real path or trail—and Dani follows. It's not long before we hit the main road, stumbling down the hillside and out of the trees. We end up on the shoulder of a two-lane highway, and it's like we're psychic or telepathic or whatever, because in unison, both Dani and I turn and head in the same direction. None of the passing cars gives us a second look. Maybe we're not worth the trouble.

Maybe we're not worth anything.

After a few minutes of walking, Dani grins and looks at me. "See how easy that was?"

I force myself to grin back but don't answer. It was easy, but disappearing's not the trick and never has been. I don't think Dani gets this yet. Her life's been filled with too many possibilities and chances and not enough rock-bottom failures, and so even though she's here it doesn't mean she *knows*.

From the day we met, I could see it in her eyes, in the way she walks. She still believes in the type of magic that tells her the world thinks she's special. That it fundamentally cares about who she is and what she does with her life, and that all the choices she makes and the battles she chooses will someday matter.

But they won't. That's the secret I hold and the truth I know. Because I have faith in a different kind of magic, a cruel and spiteful spell. It's one in which we're all forgotten eventually, and most of us are never known. But like I said, disappearing's not the trick—wanting to stay alive is.

And no one can do it forever.

"Where're we going?" Dani asks after some time has passed. I don't know how long we've been walking, really, but country roads in Georgia have a way of winding and twisting and giving the impression of progress, when, in fact, you might as well be walking in a circle.

We've passed a few clusters of homes—most are old and stately, with thick stone foundations and lots that stretch back as far as the eye can see. But there've been a couple of newer developments as well. Some gated. Some not. But no signs of impending civilization other than the buzz of passing cars. SUVs, mostly. Glossy Escalades and even a few BMWs and Mercedes. This isn't surprising. We're essentially in the extended Atlanta suburbs, and the towns out here are built for the wealthy but not by them.

"Shouldn't be too much farther," I tell her, although it's not like I have an actual destination in mind. My objective is simply to keep moving, keep living, keep existing while I'm forced to grapple with the shock and grief and rage that the morning news brought me. At the moment, however, denial's the best strategy I've got. "Hey, how was your aunt this morning? Did you two have a good breakfast?"

Dani shoots me a dark look. "Not exactly."

"Oh."

"I mean, it was awesome getting to see her. I love

Aunt Bea. She gets me in a way that my mom never has. She's also the only person in my family who's gotten away from it, you know?"

"Away from your family?"

"Yeah. But I don't mean distance-wise. She's just not like the rest of them."

"I get that," I say, although I'm not sure I do. How can any of us escape who we are? The stories that have shaped us?

"Anyway, surprise, surprise, it turns out the real reason she came was because my mom asked her to."

"Why?"

Dani kicks at a fallen tree branch lying in the shoulder of the road. "To put me in my place. It's what she does when she doesn't have control over a situation."

"How?"

"But see, that's just it. I was all ready to tell my aunt that I wanted to go. That this place isn't doing anything for me. But then my aunt tells me my mother 'isn't sure' about Peach Tree Hills. That it might not be up to her standards and she might pull me out and send me somewhere else. So suddenly everything's flipped. And instead of telling my aunt I want to leave, now I'm having to try and get her to convince my mom to let me stay because that's the only way I can have a life that's not controlled by her. It's fucked, huh? Like I can't have what I want if it's what she wants because then it's not mine."

"Huh," I say. "But does that mean you want to be here? Or do you want to leave?"

Dani throws her hands into the air. "Who the hell knows? I'm here with you, aren't I?"

"I guess you are."

"So where were you today?" she asks. "You were missing."

"I wasn't missing."

"I couldn't find you."

"I overslept."

"All day?"

"Whoa, whoa, whoa. Look at that!" I point eagerly, and Dani turns to look. Right up ahead is a sign that reads *Welcome to Leeds. Pop. 2,300.* "We made it!"

"Holy shit," Dani says, already forgetting the question she'd asked me. "We really did."

THIRTY-TWO

DANI

TOGETHER, CAMILA AND I rush forward, dirt-and-gravel shoulder turning to cobblestone walkway beneath our feet. And to my surprise, this Leeds place is a real town, complete with cute shops and boutiques and restaurants with outdoor seating. There's even a grassy park in the center that's filled with trees and play structures and people who are sunbathing and throwing Frisbees around and romping with dogs.

It's hard to describe what it's like to see people living again and being normal after two weeks stuck inside Peach Tree Hills. Talk about a shock to the system. I'm basically hypnotized by our sudden proximity to so much activity and vibrance and life. As we walk toward this giant fountain in the center of the town square, I just let my head swivel back and forth as I take in everything that's going on around me. School's definitely out, because I spot groups of teenagers lounging around, which gives me an idea. Breaking free from Camila, I bound up to one of the groups that reminds me most of my friends back home. It's the clothes they wear; the way they carry themselves.

"What's going on?" I ask.

The group eyes me with territorial skepticism, but I'm nothing if not disarming. Rather than flirt with the guys, I charm the girls, and before I know it, Camila and I are following them back to one of the girls' houses.

"Her parents are at work," I tell Camila, who's looking a little freaked-out. "Sounds like this is where they always party."

"Party?" she says.

"Let's go," I urge, and my heart is pumping overtime because, honestly, *this* is what I need right now. This is what will prove my mother wrong and my own will right. If I define my destiny, then I define myself. No one else gets to fucking do that for me.

"I don't know." Camila frowns. "That's not really what I'm into."

"Maybe it should be. Come on. It's my job to make sure you have a little fun today. I want that for you."

"Sure," she says, and I give her a hug and bump hips as we make our way through this tidy Georgia town with its perfect landscaping and blooming flowers. Then a boy—his name's

Christian—tries to talk to me, so I pull away from Camila and let him tell me the story of Leeds and how much it sucks and how his parents are both investment bankers who expect him to go to Duke or Vandy. His secret is that he wants to go to Stanford out in what his parents call Commie Californastan, but he doesn't know how to break it to them.

Lord. I may be a lot of things, but I'm not a willfully naive man-child with no sense of my place in this world. This boy, on the other hand, just might be. But he's also cute and earnest and, well, life is for the living. So in this spirit, I smile and nod and say all the right things to make him feel like there's nobility in his choices and in maybe (but probably not) being a secret sort-of liberal deep down.

Eventually we reach the girl's house, and the way everyone piles into the basement to drink and light up, it all feels so familiar. So right. The way the girls are huddled and laughing; how the boys keep arguing over music. It's like being part of a ritual, being welcomed home, but I wonder if it's also an omen of some kind. Like I've been doomed to repeat my mistakes and maybe I should try and learn better one of these days.

But I'm here, and who doesn't crave the familiar? It's instinct. It's comfort. It's knowing who I am without having to try. Besides, I've proven to everyone that I can be sober if I choose to. It wasn't even all that hard. So when I'm handed a bottle of Fireball, I take a swig. And another. And a hit of weed off the vape pen, after which I bask in the swirls of white vapor and the tingling heat of the oncoming buzz.

Camila doesn't partake, which is too bad. I try and convince her otherwise, but she's stubborn in a way that reminds me of my cousin's pug dog. The one that won't walk outside if the ground's even the slightest bit wet. It'll just fall down in the street on its side until you have to pick it up and carry it, which I guess makes the pug the smart one in this scenario. But also stubborn.

"I brought you here to have fun," I plead. "This is for you! Let yourself have something good for once."

But she just shakes her head, gloomy as ever, and well, nobody can say I didn't try. In the end, she's not my problem to worry about. On the walk over, I came up with a story about how the two of us are staying in town with an aunt for a family reunion, and even though it's possible she might tell someone something different, it's hard for me to care. What difference does it make? We'll never see these people again.

Once I'm feeling good and loose, I pull Christian into the laundry room for some making out. I'm kind of crazed for it, to have a boy touch me, want me, and as I press my lips to his, I relish in the eagerness with which his hands grip my hips and pull me to him. My head is spinning with cheap whiskey and even cheaper weed, but this is the good stuff. This is what I needed—to be wanted, physically, in a way Roger never wanted me.

Christian slides his hand up my shirt, lighting my whole

body on fire, and I fall against him. Whisper, "Let's go somewhere more private." He nods and begins walking backward, his arm fumbling for a shut door on the far end of the laundry room.

Once he gets it open, we stagger into a small powder room with a utility sink and prefab shower. The boy turns to shut the door behind us, but then lets out a startled "What the *fuck*?" and I turn and see what he sees, which is Camila huddled against the shower frame, with a broken shard of glass in one hand and what looks like blood dripping down her arm.

Fuck. *Fuck.*

"Give me your phone." Stunned, Christian tosses me his phone. "Stay with her!" I tell him, and then I return to the laundry room, where I try calling Peach Tree Hills.

This task is easier said than done, but I finally get through to the main line and beg the receptionist to put me through to one of the doctors.

"It's me, Danielle Washington. I'm a client there, and it's an emergency!" I grip the phone tight to me, heart pounding, as I peek back in the bathroom. The boy, who's kinder perhaps than I have any right to expect him to be, is sitting beside Camila, talking to her in an effort to keep her calm.

After what feels like forever, a voice comes on the line. "Tell me where you are."

"Who is this?"

"This is Dr. Roberts. Are you with Camila? We've been looking everywhere for you."

"Yes. I'm with her. That's why I'm calling. She cut herself—"

"Call 911."

"No, it's not that bad. She's not dying or anything. It's just . . . she needs to come back. We both do. She needs help. Okay?"

"Where are you?"

Of course, I have no idea, but thank God for maps and pins and technology. Once she gets the info, Dr. Roberts tells me to stay right where I am.

That help is on the way.

THIRTY-THREE

CAMILA

I HEAR THE SIRENS approaching before anyone else does. We go outside to wait, and I sit my ass on the sidewalk of this snooty upscale neighborhood while someone wraps a towel around my arm. Dani's in a whole state, staggering around and telling anyone she can about how none of this is a big deal and we'll all get together to party in the near future.

No one's buying it. I doubt even she believes what she's saying, and I end up tuning her out. It's hard to take her "oh, I'm saving this girl" act seriously because while that boy was tending to my cut, I saw her rummaging through the medicine cabinet of that bathroom. Supposedly she was looking for first-aid supplies, but she pocketed a bottle of pills when she thought I wasn't looking. So none of this was ever just "for me," and I was right about the value of friendship.

It's all self-serving.

It's all transactional.

Everything is.

Soon the wail of the sirens grows, and everyone else can hear it, too. It's fascinating how the sound overwhelms the prior serenity of the neighborhood. Suddenly people are at their windows, opening their doors, trying to get a handle on what's going on.

"Crap." Dani starts to pace, chew her nails, and I want to tell her to calm down. To let me take care of it. But when the cop car finally pulls up, lights flashing, she runs out and waves her arms, as if it's possible they wouldn't see us. I watch warily as she talks with the cops, then argues, then backs away in obvious irritation. The patrol car's passenger side door opens, and the uniformed officer who steps out is tall, broad-shouldered, and he has this paunchy stomach. All very Georgia, and not in a good way. He walks over to me, crouches down, and asks my name.

I tell him.

He asks me other things, too, and I have to show him the cut on my arm and explain that, no, I wasn't trying to end my life, I was trying to ensure I was able to keep living it. This is hard to explain, but somehow, I think he actually gets what I mean. Eventually, he tells Dani and me to get in the back of the patrol car. That he and his partner will take us back to Peach Tree Hills.

There's no resistance left in me. I slide in. Dani balks at first but relents when threatened with a breathalyzer test. Once she's in the car, she pulls her seat belt on and crosses her arms tightly.

She doesn't speak to me the whole ride.

Not once.

THIRTY-FOUR

DANI

MY ANGER STARTS TO FADE on the ride back. Yeah, it sucks having to take care of someone else when you didn't ask to, but it was naive of me not to consider how out of character Camila's been acting. I should've known I'd end up having to be the adult when shit went sideways.

The cops pull into the Peach Tree Hills driveway, and I groan when I see the crowd that's waiting for us. Even some of the other girls are watching, and honestly, they look pissed. I'm still a little buzzed, so it's easy to pretend we're movie stars pulling up to the waiting paparazzi, and because I'm a total bitch, I do a pageant wave from the back seat.

Once parked, the officer gets out, opens the car door, and

releases us to our captors. At the same time, Dr. Sánchez marches up to shake the officer's hand and starts kissing his ass about how grateful she is that they've returned us to the place we tried to flee.

Yolanda's the first to approach Camila and me. Her usually smiling face clouded with fury, she grabs us both, only to be stopped by Camila's howl of pain.

She quickly releases her. "What's the matter?"

"It's her arm," I tell her. "She hurt it."

"Let me see," Yolanda snaps.

Camila writhes backward, out of reach. "It's just a scratch."

"Show me."

After shooting a murderous glare at all the girls who've gathered to watch, Camila finally relents and pulls up her shirtsleeve to reveal an admittedly shallow but gruesome-looking cut. It's not bleeding too much anymore, but the area's oozy and all the surrounding skin is red and angry-looking.

"How'd it happen?" Yolanda asks.

Camila glances at me. "A glass broke, and I was trying to pick up the pieces."

"Let me get someone to look at it. You're going to need stitches." The three of us head inside the main administrative building and walk briskly back to the medical area. Yolanda uses her key card to open an exam room for Camila and then shuts the door before hustling off to find a nurse. I know it's only a matter of time before someone's sent in to yell at me, so I sit in the waiting area and poke around at the magazines, which are all geared toward wellness practices and total mind-body health, whatever fresh hell that might be.

The photos are gross. Mostly slim women in their thirties doing yoga or sipping tea or playing with a golden retriever. Also, they've had their nipples and labia photoshopped out of existence, transforming the images into something creepy in this uncanny-valley kind of way that makes my skin crawl.

I put the magazines back down and try and remember what it was like having Christian touch me, the way my body felt pressed up against his. It's hard to concentrate, though. My head's starting to hurt and my legs keep jittering, and I can't stop thinking about what's coming next. I don't mean confrontation. Adults always rage when you don't do what they want you to. It's pretty much the only way to get a genuine reaction out of them. Besides, I've been in trouble before. Plenty of times.

That's not what's bothering me.

After a few minutes, I hop to my feet, walk to the water fountain, and pour myself a cup of water. It's refreshingly cold, and I kind of have the urge to dump a second cup on my head. Before I can do this, however, I spot a young woman in a white doctor's coat walking swiftly down the hall.

"Hey." I step in front of her, stopping the woman in her tracks. I recognize her as Camila's doctor.

"Yes." She tries peering around me, eager to get where she's going.

"You're going to see Camila, right?" I ask.

"I can't speak with you about that."

"Well, I'm the one who was with her earlier. I talked to you on the phone, and I know what happened."

The doctor blinks. "Okay."

I take a deep breath. "Look, she didn't cut herself on broken glass. I mean, she did, but it wasn't an accident. She did it on purpose."

"You're sure about that?"

"I saw her do it."

"What else did you see?"

"That's it. I just thought you should know."

The doctor thanks me, and I watch her continue down the hall toward the exam room where Camila's waiting, and then I just stand there feeling guilty and terrible because I don't know what to do with myself and also I don't know if I've done the right thing or not.

What if I haven't?

"Danielle," a voice calls out.

I turn and see Yolanda. She gestures for me to follow her, which I do, but I stop when she tries waving me into the second exam room.

"But I'm not hurt," I tell her.

"Have a seat," she insists, and once I'm in the room, she starts opening cabinet doors and looking around. "Dr. Allegheny ordered some tests for you, so we have to do them."

"What tests?"

She retrieves something from a bottom shelf. "Urine and blood."

"Are you kidding me?"

"Nope." She stands with a grunt, cheeks suddenly red, and hands me the urine specimen cup. "You want to take care of that first? Bathroom's down the hall on your left. I'll do the blood draw when I get back."

I feel sick. "Dr. *Allegheny* ordered this?"

"That's right."

"Jesus." I snatch the cup from her hand. "This is so insulting."

Her jaw tightens. "So's running away to party without letting anyone know where you are. Do you know how scary that was for us?"

"*I* brought us back," I tell her. "I'm the one who did that."

"Fine."

I open the door, step into the hallway, and come face-to-face with Camila.

Her eyes narrow at the sight of me.

"Hey," I say tentatively.

"Fuck off," she says before brushing past me, disappearing

down the hall. Stunned, I just stand there, unable to process what just happened.

"You okay?"

I turn and see Yolanda watching me closely. But I don't answer her. Instead, still gripping the specimen cup in one hand, I swipe at my eyes with the other before straightening my spine, throwing back my shoulders, and marching to the bathroom.

Later, I have to sit outside our dorm room while Dr. Roberts and Yolanda search the place. I'm not sure what they're looking for exactly, but they find something under Camila's mattress. My guess is that it's a knife or something because I can hear them talking about her cutting, which, other than today, is not something I've seen her do. Although, when I think back on it, she did get freaked when I came in the room that one time. She said it was about dancing, not wanting me to see her dance, but I don't know.

Maybe it was something else.

When they're finished, I'm allowed to go back in, and they remind me that I can't leave the room or go anywhere but the bathroom without permission.

"Whatever," I say because I'm exhausted and I can't stop thinking about the anger in Camila's eyes when I saw her in the hall earlier. No one likes a snitch, and no good deed goes unpunished. I don't blame her. But I also think I was right to tell her doctor what I knew. Seeing her like that, with all that blood . . .

I shudder, then rush to the window. When I finally spot Yolanda and Dr. Roberts walking back across the courtyard, I pull the pill bottle from my pocket. Invasive procedures aside, no one bothered to search my clothes, which is laughable. Pouring them out into my cupped palm, I count quickly. Thirty. I've got thirty Vicodin, and believe me when I say the urge is strong to take one. But I don't. I'll need to be clear-headed when Camila returns or else she'll snitch on me as revenge.

But this gives me an idea. After returning the pills to the bottle and securing the lid, I head to the closet, which has a built-in plastic clothes rod and a handful of plastic hangers attached to it that can't be removed without taking off the whole rod. The whole thing's flimsy and cheap-looking, but I guess the idea is to let us have clothes but also not let us have any items we could hurt ourselves with. Anyway, the point is that the plastic rod itself is hollow, and with a little light force, I'm able to pry it away from the wall on one side and slide the pills right in. Then I shove the rod back and feel a surge of pride at my accomplishment.

Hell, forget necessity. Around here, paranoia's the mother of invention.

THIRTY-FIVE

CAMILA

THE WORST THING about all of this is that I'm forced to talk to my parents on the phone. It's not clear if they insisted or if the staff at Peach Tree Hills did, but the fact of the matter is that no one bothered to ask what *I* want.

Dr. Roberts sits with me during the call.

"Hello," I say.

"Camila! Sweetie, are you okay?" It's my mother, her voice as familiar and warm as ever. Something in me feels physically sick hearing it and suddenly wanting so badly to be close to her. But this is how nostalgia and memory work, how they team up to manipulate my emotions and get me to surrender in times when strength is called for.

"I'm fine," I say stiffly. "I know what I did was wrong. I shouldn't have done it. I'm sorry for all the trouble I've caused."

"We're not worried about that, baby," my father jumps in. "We just want to know if you're okay. If you're getting the help you need. We love you, Cams. More than anything. And we know this isn't an easy time for you, especially considering . . ."

"I'm fine," I say again.

"Is it true you cut yourself?" my mother asks.

"It's nothing bad. Just a scratch. I didn't even need stitches."

"Why'd you do it? Why would you do that?"

"It's not the first time, Mama. You know that."

"But you said you'd stopped. You promised."

"Well, what did you think I'd say?" I snap. "Did you think I'd tell you the truth just so you could make me feel worse about it?"

Of course, she starts crying after this, and of course, it's impossible not hate myself. I didn't have to respond like that or use that tone, but I'm tired of having to hide who I really am. I'm tired of everything, really.

My dad takes the phone. "They told us you ran away."

"We didn't run away. We just left for a little while. We always meant to come back."

"You left without telling anyone."

"It wasn't a big deal."

"Lying's a big deal, Cams. You know that."

"You're one to talk," I say because it's not like he's honest about his problems. His own dark moods and brittle sorrow.

"What's that supposed to mean?" he asks.

"Nothing. Forget it."

His voice lowers. "No matter what happens to us in this life, our integrity is all we've got. Don't let anyone take that from you, sweetie. You've always been true to yourself. It's what I love about you and what makes you special. I don't know who this roommate of yours is, but don't let her change you."

I roll my eyes. "There's no chance of that happening, Daddy. Trust me. I'll probably be in lockdown for the rest of the time. Solitary confinement or something."

"I just want you to remember who you are."

"I'm not the one who's forgotten."

"We should talk about Fieldbrook," he says.

"No."

"Your mother and I, we both wished we could've talked with you beforehand. We discussed that with Dr. Sánchez, but with the deadline coming up and the messages we were getting . . ."

"I don't want to talk about that. Not now. Or ever. There's no point. Just forget it."

"I know you're upset with us, but you have to understand that we made this decision with your best interest in mind. We can't stand to see you hurt yourself. And now with you cutting again, well, we really can't take any chances—"

I hang up the phone. There are some things I can't do, either.

Dr. Roberts looks at me. "How'd it go?"

I glare at her. "Awful."

"Is there anything I can do?"

"Yeah," I say. "Don't make me talk to them ever again."

THIRTY-SIX

DANI

"IT'S NOT FAIR," I tell Dr. Allegheny when I see him the following morning. "None of it was my idea. Camila's the one who wanted to leave, and I just went with her. And then I'm the one who got us back safely, but now she's being treated like some special princess and I keep getting yelled at and having to take drug tests."

"Is that really how you understand what's happened?" he asks.

"You see it differently?"

"Your roommate and her concerns aside, you willingly left the property without letting anyone know where you were going. You drank alcohol and smoked weed. You attended a party with people you don't know. Your poor judgment and impulsiveness don't reflect a lot of progress on your part."

But that's the point, I want to say. Instead I go with: "How'd you know about the party?"

"The cops reported it."

"Oh, well, that was some other bullshit, by the way." I sit up straight. "I called here for help, and you people sent *cops* to come and get us? Two brown girls in a rich Georgia suburb? Come on. You have to know that's a bad idea. It's lucky we didn't end up dead. My mom would've sued this place out of existence if anything had happened."

"I share your concern about that," he says. "I do, and it wasn't my call. It's also something I've brought up with the administration."

"Really?"

"Yes. Unfortunately, in the state of Georgia, if an individual is deemed a danger to themselves and in need of hospitalization, transport must be done by law enforcement. Once it was reported that your roommate had cut herself, they had to be sent out, and we have a good relationship with the Leeds police department. They have better training than most when it comes to mental health. But"—he holds a hand up to keep me from jumping in—"but that doesn't mean it couldn't have been handled differently, and I do apologize for that."

"Thank you," I tell him grudgingly. "I appreciate it."

"Can we get back to talking about you? It sounds like you're pretty angry with your roommate for putting you in such a challenging position."

I slouch down in my chair. "I'm not really mad at her. I'm more worried than anything. She was really weird, though, the whole time. The way she was acting."

"How so?"

"I don't know. She doesn't talk about things. I thought she was having a good time. . . . We were just getting out for a couple of hours. I really had every intention of coming back. But it's fun to break the rules every now and then. There's no harm in that. It just feels good, you know?"

"How is it fun to break rules?" he asks.

"How else do you know you're alive? Unless, you know, you're the one making the rules."

He nods. "I see."

"And yeah, I drank a little. Smoked a little. It wasn't anything out of control, though. Just some partying."

"What was your roommate doing while you were partying?"

I tilt my head. "She doesn't drink, if that's what you're asking."

"That wasn't my question."

"I don't know what she was doing. Talking to people, I guess? Hanging out. Being normal?"

"You saw this?"

"No. I'm not her babysitter. She's a big girl. She was the one who wanted to go out and have an adventure in the first place, and that's what we did."

"How much did you drink?"

"Couple of shots."

"A couple?"

"Four or five. And I took a couple hits off a joint."

"Anything else?"

"No."

"On a scale of one to ten, how likely do you think it would be that, if given the same opportunity, you'd drink again?"

"Ten being the most likely?"

"That's right?"

I think about this. "Eight, probably."

"And if you were not here, but instead, say, back at home, how often would such an opportunity arise in your normal life?"

"I mean, I could find a party every day if I wanted to."

"Would you want to?"

"No. That's too much."

"So in an ideal but average week, how many parties would you seek out?"

"Maybe one to two tops. I've got other things going on that I'm involved in. Model UN. This public art advocacy program. The lit mag. I'm pretty ambitious, you know."

"So, again, on a scale of one to ten, how important is it to you to fulfill your other commitments, like Model UN, the art advocacy project, and other activities that you enjoy?"

"Ten," I say.

He writes something down. "That's helpful to know. I do hear what you're saying about wanting to break the rules in order to feel in control of your life. But it also sounds as if you have a lot of other passions and interests that you find fulfilling and that you're committed to pursuing."

"Is that so notable? Isn't that what everyone's like?"

"Not necessarily."

"I had no idea."

Dr. Allegheny smiles.

"Is this where you tell me how I have to get sober or else I'll die in a gutter?"

"No," he says. "However, I would like to discuss your aunt's visit yesterday, but we're out of time at the moment. Let's pick up there tomorrow."

"So I'm not in trouble?" I ask.

"I didn't say that. But not with me."

"Figures." I sigh. "Camila and I are meeting with Dr. Sánchez at eleven. She stayed in the infirmary last night, though, so I haven't even seen her."

"I know about the meeting," he says.

"She's mad at me. Did you know that, too? I try and help

the girl, get in trouble for my effort, and now she won't even talk to me!"

Dr. Allegheny lifts an eyebrow. "How do you understand her anger?"

"She's probably mad that I snitched on her for cutting. Which I get. But I didn't know what else to do."

"You did the right thing, Danielle."

"Says you. Anyway, I should probably be the one that's angry. I think the whole reason she wanted to leave yesterday was to . . . you know, do what she did."

"Hurt herself?"

I nod. "That was hard to see. It was bad."

"Are you okay?" he asks.

"I think so. I've always been good in a crisis. Even when I'm fucked-up. I don't know why that is."

"You did the right thing," he says again.

"I know. But like I said, she doesn't see it that way."

"Do you think there might be other reasons for her anger?"

"Like what?" I ask.

"Like maybe the two of you aren't so different after all."

The meeting takes places in one of the big conference rooms—the one where I was supposed to do that worthless drug assessment, which feels like forever ago.

Today, when I step inside the room, I'm filled with apprehension. Dread, too. Seated around the table are Dr. Sánchez, Dr. Roberts, Yolanda, and a counselor I don't recognize. Camila's there, too, obviously, looking fragile and precious with her tiny arm bandaged up and a glass of orange juice in front of her. Nobody passes me any juice, and the truth couldn't be more evident: Camila's going to get to be the victim today.

I've been cast as the villain.

"First things first," Dr. Sánchez says in that stern voice of hers, and I can't help but stare at her makeup. Her eyebrows are so sharp and perfectly shaped, it's almost as if she isn't real. "What happened yesterday was unacceptable. From a safety standpoint. From a personal responsibility standpoint. And possibly a legal one."

"Legal?"

"You're minors," she snaps. "And you're under our care and representing our facility. Do you think the town of Leeds is thrilled over this incident? Or your parents?"

"You think I care about the town of *Leeds*?"

"We're sorry," Camila says from the opposite side of the table. "Well, I am, at least."

"Traitor," I mutter.

Dr. Sánchez sighs. "Thank you, Camila. But an apology doesn't change the fact that you chose to leave this property and that you both broke numerous rules that you were well aware of when you broke them. If you are to remain in our care, you're going to need to abide by additional security restrictions to ensure your ongoing safety and the safety of our other guests."

"Are you going to make us wear ankle bracelets?" I ask tartly.

The looks she gives me is not a friendly one. "I don't think you appreciate our position here. You are in our care. This is a medical setting, to a certain extent, and there is a great deal of responsibility that your parents have entrusted us with, as well as the surrounding communities. Peach Tree Hills was developed as a transitional housing opportunity for girls who could benefit from our clinical services but who were currently stable and otherwise not in imminent danger and able to engage in therapy and school and community building. We've never had to worry about significant security breaches because no one's ever broken our trust in this way."

I stare at the table. "Look, I *get* it."

"Do you?"

"I just said I did. And I am sorry. I know we did something shitty."

The woman I spoke with on the phone—Dr. Roberts— jumps in. "First of all, you should know that we've been in touch with your parents to inform them about what's happened."

I roll my eyes at this. "Okay. What did they say?"

"They stated a desire for you to stay here and to continue your work toward recovery. I expressed my gratitude that they're able to see the bigger picture."

"I think you mean the empty nest," I quip.

Camila's lips twitch in response, but Yolanda is unamused. "From now on, you will be under our highest level of supervision. No more free time on the property, and you'll have an aide accompanying you between activities.

"Additionally, because we believe in restorative justice—not punishment—you two will be working with me over the next two weeks and finding ways to enhance our community through collaboration and positive action."

"What does *that* mean?" I ask.

"Good question, Dani. Well, today you're going to spend the afternoon cleaning out our lost and found. In addition to a big clean, the whole space needs organizing and the shelves require new labels and storage containers. The rest is TBD, but I'm open to suggestions."

I scowl. "Sounds like punishment to me."

"It's not."

Camila squirms in her chair. "Lost and found? You mean you want us to go through other people's stuff?"

"That's right."

"Can't I do something else?" Camila pleads. "I'll work in the garden. I don't like dust."

"We have masks you can wear."

"Does that mean it's a health hazard?"

"No."

"What about the garden?" she insists.

"It's not an option," Yolanda snaps.

"Well, I don't want to work with her." Camila jerks her head in my direction. "I don't want to live with her anymore, either."

"Poor you," I say.

"Ladies," Dr. Sánchez cuts in. "None of this is negotiable, and you certainly haven't earned the right to compromise. Personally, I thought you should've both been dismissed from our program. Rules are rules. But other people thought . . . differently. So here we are. You can take this offer, or we can make arrangements for your return home."

"This is doing a lot for my recovery." Camila holds up her bandaged arm.

"The real punishment is working with her, right?" I ask.

Yolanda appears ready to throttle us both. "I'll meet you this afternoon at two in the courtyard. I'll have the key and any supplies you might you need."

"Fine," I mutter.

"What if I don't feel safe?" Camila asks.

"What're you talking about?"

"She's not trustworthy."

"That's really not the point of this task, Camila."

"Then what is the point?"

This I can answer.

"Don't you see?" I tell her. "The point is for us to feel bad."

THIRTY-SEVEN

CAMILA

I SQUEEZE MY EYES SHUT, tight as I can, and will my body elsewhere. Anywhere. Somewhere.

I'm denied, as always, and so I listen to the screeching call of a crow, the creak and moan of tree branches overhead girding themselves against the wind, the faint hum of the highway from many miles away, and when I open my eyes, I'm still here. I'm still rooted in the same spot I've been standing in for twenty minutes—directly in front of the locked yoga studio.

I reach for and try the door.

Still locked.

"Hey," a voice says, causing me to look over my shoulder. Two girls are behind me. I've seen them before but don't know their names. Or maybe I do. My head's still hazy with the extra medication I've been given, especially last night in the clinic, where I stayed under observation until I was trusted to leave. Well, not trusted, exactly. A nurse's aide has been shadowing me ever since, although at the moment, he's keeping a respectful distance.

"Hey," I say to the girls. They're both younger than I am. Maybe thirteen? Fourteen? That hint of baby softness lingers in their faces, their expressions, and it threatens to break my heart. I was their age once but never will be again, and these are the truths I'm meant to accept. That this is what it means to live and also die.

"It's true, right?" one of the girls says.

"Is what true?"

"That you're going to be a famous dancer. We watched one of your videos online."

"You did? One of my videos?"

The girl nods. "You were in Louisville. You won first place dancing to a Taylor Swift song. You looked really pretty, too."

The memory of that weekend floats back to me. My mama cheering in the crowd when they called my name. I wonder what she would think if she could see these girls talking about it. A moment that had brought her such pride. "Pretty, huh?"

She nods.

"Where'd you see it?" I ask, since we're not able to access YouTube or any social media site in the computer lab. "Where was it posted?"

The two girls look at each other, sharing some secret glance that I'm not privy to. It's very sisterly and private, but I don't mind. Everyone deserves their own secrets.

Except me, apparently.

"Never mind," I tell them, scowling at the nurse's aide, who's now sitting at a picnic table. "It's true. That was me. I love dancing. Not sure about the famous part, though."

"I heard you were going to some fancy dance academy."

My mouth sours. "No."

"Oh."

The second girl, the one who hasn't spoken yet, suddenly pipes up. "I take dance lessons back home. Tap, mostly."

"How long?" I ask.

"Since I was six."

"Nice. You any good?"

She blushes. "Jenny Roycroft's better."

"Fuck Jenny Roycroft," I say.

The girl startles, then laughs. "Yeah, sure."

"Hey, we gotta go," the first girl says. "Group starts in five."

"Okay," says the second girl. "Thanks, Camila."

"For what?"

She makes a goofy face. "I don't know."

They scurry off, arm in arm, a picture of such harmony and mutual trust that it whips my own resentment back into focus. Nothing about this life is fair, least of all the fact that even when you work hard to keep your distance from other people, they can still stab you in the back.

They can still betray you.

And, in fact, they will.

Soon the bell rings, signaling the top of the hour with its heavy clang of metal and motion and beckoning me to the court-yard so that I can start my penance and seek forgiveness I never asked for in the first place. Resistance is an illusion, and as I walk toward my stated destination, the aide following me like an unwanted shadow, I'm struck by the familiarity of my actions, like a dream long gone or the faint shimmer of déjà vu. This is who I am and who I've always been. I comply.

I comply.

I comply.

By the time I get there, Dani and Yolanda are already standing by the picnic tables, their bodies relaxed and unbothered, even in the late-spring heat. They don't see me coming, not at first, but when they do, they quickly stop talking, which means they were talking about me.

"Let's get this over with." I stand to the side, hands in my pockets.

"That's the plan," Dani says brightly.

Yolanda waves to my aide—aka my babysitter—and tells him he can go to lunch. Then she looks at me and forces a smile in a way that makes me think she must really hate me. "Danielle has the key, and I've already told her how to access the room and where the cleaning supplies are. There are some garbage bags in there, but we'll probably need to do a dump run over the weekend, so you can just pile anything obviously broken or damaged on the brick walkway outside the building itself. We'll do the rest."

"You aren't going to be with us?" I ask.

"No," she says briskly. "I have other stuff to do."

"But I thought someone was going to monitor our every move."

"I trust you two to work together responsibly."

"Why?" I say. "We're not trustworthy."

"I'll be sure to check up on you in regular intervals, then."

"Nice going," Dani says once Yolanda's walked away and is out of earshot. "Great job ensuring more surveillance."

"You know, I didn't sign up to be lectured at," I snap.

"Well, I didn't sign up for any of this."

"Lie," I say. "Total lie. In fact, you might be the only girl here who *did* sign up for this whole experience. Just to get out of your mommy's house because you think it's mean when she doesn't agree with you."

Dani stiffens. "I'm not having this discussion with you."

"Oh, so now you don't have anything to say."

"I am choosing not to engage. Also, come on. You need to follow me."

"Why do I have to follow you?"

"Because I'm the one who actually knows where we're going!"

I roll my eyes, but no one's around to see it. And then, yeah, I do follow after her.

Of course I do.

That's how pathetic I am.

THIRTY-EIGHT

DANI

CAMILA IS STOMPING after me like a petulant child. She really hates that I'm the one with the key, and even more, she hates that I'm the one who ratted her out. I *get* it. But I also didn't do anything wrong.

At least I don't think I did.

The lost and found is located within this single-story utility-and-storage building located on the far side of the property. We have to walk down the hill from the vegetable garden and all the way to the edge of the meadow. It seems like we could just make another run for it if we wanted to brave the wilderness, but maybe it's clear we don't.

Want to, that is.

Once Camila spots the building, her quick strides pull her in front of me. Jesus, the girl is seriously pissed. I can see it in her movements, all snap and rhythm and spite. Wasted effort, if you ask me. We're going to do *chores*. That's not something where it pays to be first past the post, but I just let her do her thing. I watch as she hustles her butt away from me only to feel a smug pang of satisfaction when she finally reaches the locked door and has to wait for me to get there.

"You knew I had the key," I tell her, but once I've got the place unlocked, I pull open the door and let her in first.

I follow right behind. As we step inside the building, curiosity swiftly consumes us both. This place is *strange*. It's also gloomy, dark, and full of dust—but mostly strange.

I creep down a narrow aisle of metal prefab shelving—the kind you see in garages and probably buy in bulk at a big box store. Even in grainy darkness, I can see that each shelf is packed tight with an odd assortment of items. Shoes and furniture and stuffed animals and mugs and books and posters and stacks of DVDs and piles of headphones. There's even a banged-up PlayStation and something that looks like one of those old-fashioned popcorn poppers that you're supposed to hold over an open fire.

Peering between the shelves, I make out what looks like endless rows of shelving but must be an optical illusion of some kind. Because the shelves stretch as far as I can see, which is weird, since the room's dimensions appeared modest from the outside. But from in here, the place is cavernous.

I weave my way over to the next aisle. These shelves are crowded with boxes and clear plastic bins that mostly contain clothing. I dig through a few, looking for something fun, but there's a non-zero amount of underwear and also nothing appears to be all that clean, so I shove it all back in the box with a shudder and retreat to the first aisle, which is where I find Camila also pawing through various items.

I have no clue what we're supposed to be cleaning, but I also don't care. I pull a storage box down and open it. Inside is a bunch of grubby clothing that includes such treasures as a single flip-flop. The thing is, there's actually a label on the plastic bin that reads *Amelia D,* and also there's a tacky framed photograph in there featuring a picture of a boy and a puppy.

An item on a lower shelf catches my eye. It's a music box. The room's minimal light glints off the brass gears, and I pull it toward me, somewhat startled by its heft. The base is carved from wood, and atop it rests a tall porcelain ballerina in a red dress who's holding her arms above her head for all eternity. I cradle her carefully but then look back at the storage box I'd just opened. Amelia's storage box.

I frown. "Hold on. Do they actually know who all this stuff belongs to?"

Camila doesn't look up. "Some of it, I guess."

"Well, then why don't they just send those items back? Why keep it here?"

This is when she crumples. Not physically or anything, but something inside of her gives up. The first crack comes in the trembling of her lips. The sorrow in her eyes. Then I get it. I understand what she's reacting to and why she's worried that maybe there's no girl to send the belongings back to anymore.

"Oh God." I go to her and wrap my arms around her. "Come here. I'm sorry, Cams. I'm so, so sorry."

She presses her face to my chest, and for a moment, I absorb the heat of her tears. Her pain. But then she pushes back and sits up, using her good arm to wipe her cheeks, her nose.

"I'm okay," she says. "I'm fine."

"You don't have to be," I say.

"I know." Her eyes are all pink. "I'm sorry, too. For yesterday. For scaring you like I did. I never meant for that to happen."

I don't say anything. I'm not sure if she's saying she's sorry for what she did or if she's sorry I found out.

"You want to know why I was upset? Why I wanted to leave in the first place?"

"Sure," I say.

"My therapist. I met with her yesterday, and she said my parents had called. They'd found out about some of the emails I'd been sending out, including the one to my local dance company. I guess this upset them. I'm not sure why. But they told her they'd contacted Fieldbrook Academy and declined my admission on my behalf."

"Fuck." I stare at Camila. "That's really, really shitty that they did that."

"Yeah, it is." She sighs. "I wasn't trying to kill myself yesterday, though. I just . . . It's something I do when I'm stressed, and it's fine. I mean, it's not a good thing, but I know why you told my doctor, and it's not a big deal or anything. It's sort of a relief on account of I should've told her sooner how I was feeling. But it's not easy to talk about, and well, I just thought you should know that."

"I get it," I tell her. "Or at least I think I do."

She looks up. "Yeah?"

I nod. "Sort of. I had a boyfriend back home who used to hurt himself."

Camila smiles. "A boyfriend?"

"Ex," I say quickly. "He sold me out to my parents."

"Oh."

"But I think I get what you mean. About stress. And it not being easy to talk about."

"Even though all we do is talk around here." She sighs. "I don't even know what's so hard about talking. It's more like, when people ask questions, they take part of you if you answer them. Do you know what I mean?"

"Maybe. Like a control thing?"

"Not exactly." She scrunches her nose up, then points at the music box I've still got clutched in my arms. "What's that?"

"I thought you'd like it." I shove it toward her. "She kind of looks like you, don't you think?"

Camila reaches to turn the music box key, winding up the gears. When she releases it, a tinny song floats through the air, and she sets the whole thing on the floor between us, where we watch the dancer spin on her toes.

After a moment, Camila reaches for something I hadn't noticed earlier. But there's a drawer in the base of the box that's been sealed shut with a thin piece of tape. I grip the base as she pulls again, and it finally pulls open. Flies open, really. Right into Camila's hands.

She laughs. "Look at this."

I peer around the dancer. Inside the drawer is a pile of envelopes wrapped in a lacy white ribbon. On top of the stack is a small green Post-it with the words *read me* scrawled across it.

"Weird," I say. "What are those?"

"I don't know." Camila tugs the ribbon off and holds up the top envelope, inspecting it all over. Nothing identifying's written on it, but there appears to be a letter inside.

"What should I do?" she says.

"Just what the note says," I tell her. "Read them."

THIRTY-NINE

CAMILA

Dear Mikell,

You wouldn't believe what it's like in here. I don't even think I'm supposed to be writing to you, so it might as well be a prison, although they don't call it that. But function follows form, right? We're not supposed to have contact with the outside world, and this is supposed to be somehow "therapeutic" and not "cruel and unusual punishment"?

Anyway, it's shit like this that gets to me and makes me feel like I'm being brainwashed. Not in a Manchurian candidate kind of way. I'm not totally paranoid. But it's still infuriating when stuff like phone calls and letters and television are dangled as enticements for "good behavior." They've already taken away everything we care about, and so they know our dependence is a foregone conclusion. It's just a sick cycle, and I wish they could just be honest about it.

In a way, the system reminds me of that book they made us read back in ninth grade where the government convinces people that they want to give up their rights in the name of safety and security, but for the life of me, I can't remember the title. My mind's pretty foggy these days. But the point is that I hate it here, and the worst part is that I agreed to come.

I think I just didn't know what else to do after everything that happened, and well, you know what that looked like. It's hard when you hurt so many people. It's hard to believe in anything, including yourself. Maybe this is all I deserve. Maybe it's more.

Anyway, I'd better go now. I mostly want you to know that I miss you. I hate that I can't be there, and also tell baby Georgie hello from me. Scratch behind his ears. He likes that.

—K

Dear Mikell,

You wouldn't believe this shrink they're making me see. You'd hate her. She's worse than when we had Mrs. Gómez that year we took computer science. Remember how strict she was? And how she didn't believe we actually knew anything?

Anyway, that's what this doctor is like. Highly skeptical

about things she knows nothing about. And lucky me, I have to talk to her every day for at least an hour. Also she does this pursed little butthole mouth thing anytime she doesn't like what you're saying. For me she does this whenever I talk about how therapy doesn't help and how I think forcing someone to take medication against their will ought to be illegal. I told her torture went against the Geneva Conventions and that she could be jailed as a war criminal.

"What war?" she asked me, and I was only half kidding when I told her it was the war on childhood. But I know we've talked about it before. How society punishes the youth for being young. How we're not allowed to dream.

Who wouldn't want to be mad in such circumstances?
Who wouldn't want to lead the rebellion?
Fight on,
-K

Dear Mikell,

It's been a while since I wrote last and even longer since I've been able to send anything out or connect with the world around me. I've been in contact with some people, obviously. My family came out and visited once, including Carson and Valerie.

They came twice, actually, since I'm not sure I told you about the first time, which was god-awful. We had to do this family session where my mom kept crying and wailing about how she was blamed for my failures and how guilty she felt. I haven't been that angry in a long time, which is a testament to the drugs they're giving me in here. They make all my problems feel a little bit distant. Like maybe someone else is taking care of them for a while.

But the thing that got me while my mom was freaking out was that poor Carson and Valerie were stuck in that room playing with this crummy dollhouse while they had to listen to her spew that bullshit. I could tell they were both doing their best to pretend they weren't there. That's the beauty of being ten — there's still magic on this earth.

But magic doesn't last forever. Is that why adolescence is so sucky? You have to accept this new reality while adults are doing all they can to get you to forfeit your grief and pretend it didn't matter when they crushed your dreams. But I remember and I miss you, Mikell. I wish like hell everything hadn't gone down the way it did, and I wish I'd done something to stop what was going on with Bark and Kaye and all that. I should've told you that. I should've done a lot of things, and you probably should've, too. But I'm not mad. I'm just thinking a lot about it all. I just wanted you to know.

-K

Dani puts down the letter and looks at me. "These are intense. Why are they just in here?"

"I don't know."

She stretches and looks around the room. The light's changed, with the sunlight not falling against the back wall. "What time do you think it is? We haven't cleaned anything."

"Oh well. What's Yolanda going to do about it? Make us not clean out the lost-and-found room?"

Dani grins. "When did you stop giving fucks?"

"She's the worst. Because she pretends like she's our friend."

"I don't get a friend vibe from her, really. She's just working for the institution and not us. It's in her best interest not to rock the boat."

"God, I hate that phrase," I say. "*Don't rock the boat.* It's like my parents' excuse for everything. They don't fight to make things better. They'd just rather give up."

"I want to keep reading!" Dani whines.

"Who do you think Mikell is?" I ask.

She scans the letters again. "Is he her brother?"

"I don't think so. He would've visited with her family. But I don't think he's a boyfriend, either, though."

"So just a friend?"

I shrug. "I guess."

"Read the next one," Dani implores. "Read it out loud."

So I do:

Dear Mikell,

Today was the worst day ever. I've literally done everything they've asked of me here. I play the part of the good robot. I take my meds. Go to therapy. Do my little watercolors in art class and pretend I'm inspired.

Well, what good has any of that been? Today was my official "check-in" with my treatment team, and do you know what they told me? They said I haven't been exhibiting any "prosocial" behaviors and that I have to stay here for at least another six weeks! Mom and Dad signed off on this, and if I wasn't the black sheep of the family before, I definitely am now. Everything gets blamed on my problems. Even the accident's my fault now, despite the fact I wasn't there and they *know* that.

My roommate's dealing with some similar shit, so at least I have someone to talk to. Well, not exactly the same, but her older sister died last fall after contracting a virus in college. Meningitis, I think. But the similar part is that her sister was her parents' favorite. The golden girl. She was at Georgetown, and her parents took money from the other kids' college fund to pay for her to go because they said she was the smartest and deserved the opportunity. And it killed her. Can you imagine?

By the way, I have a formal diagnosis now. I thought I'd be labeled a sociopath or something, but my shrink called it a "conduct disorder" compounded with "traumatic grief." The grief I get, but the conduct stuff is bullshit. Apparently it's based on whether or not someone is willing to follow the rules in a society, not whether or not those rules are oppressive or cruel or unfair. That's what no one is willing to consider. That maybe I'm not bad for the sake of being bad. I'm bad for the sake of survival.

Fuck. I know you understand this, and I'm so sorry for all you've been through the same way I feel sorry for myself. In a way, being in here has been an opportunity to reflect on what I believe in and what it means to fight for those beliefs. I guess the good thing is that there are a few people here who understand me, even if the staff isn't interested in my ideas or how I really feel. Well, they're interested but to a *point*. What they aren't interested in is changing themselves. Most people are like that, I guess. Lazy. But I refuse to change and grow up and uphold the status quo just because it's easier.

I promise to always fight. To always value the underdog.

Do you remember that time in third or fourth grade when we took a field trip to that park by the water and we got nets to try and catch butterflies so we could study them? You were so sad about the whole thing. Like, you already knew how beautiful the butterflies were without killing them. Or you knew that killing something beautiful was something only ugly people did.

Anyway, I just remember how distraught you were by the whole situation while everyone else was laughing and running around and having the best goddamn time of their lives. That's a little what being here reminds me of. Does that make sense? It's like everyone's doing all this work and therapy and validating each other about finding the joy in life and building relationships that matter and all that. But I can only see the futility of their efforts. Like, it's obvious life is going to destroy most of these girls. Life destroys most girls, I think. But being here feels like watching butterflies be oblivious to the net. Like I'm the only one who sees the real danger, and it's breaking me, Mikell. That's what I want you to know. I understand how you felt that day because it's how I feel every day.

Keep fighting. Or maybe that should be: Keep your tenderness. Just hold it close. Okay?

-K

FORTY

DANI

WE'RE NOT EVEN halfway through the letters when Yolanda returns and tells us we have to lock up and head back for dinner.

"What time is it?" I ask.

"Almost five."

I give a low whistle. "Damn, that flew by."

She takes a step inside the room and looks around disapprovingly. "Because you were getting so much work done?"

"We got a slow start," I say.

"You'll have time tomorrow," she says. "I wouldn't worry too much about it."

Camila grips the letters and the music box. "Can we keep these? Please?"

Yolanda frowns. "What are they?"

"They're these old letters we found," I say. "There's no name on them. Just an initial."

"And you want to bring them to your room?"

Camila nods.

She sighs. "Why don't you leave the music box here for now. It's not going anywhere. The letters . . . I guess they're okay to take, but be careful with them. They belong to someone."

"Well, that's why we should keep them," Camila says cheerfully. "So we can figure whose they are. There're clues in here that would help us find her. Whoever she is. She'd probably want them back."

"Is there a question in there?" Yolanda asks.

"How could we find out who wrote them? Is there someone here who might know? Maybe Dr. Sánchez?"

"I can ask around," she says. "But no promises. I said you could take the letters, but I'm not looking to get involved in your Nancy Drew mystery."

Camila thanks her, but I can tell that Yolanda's uncomfortable with the situation somehow. Like maybe she's picking up on the same thing I am with Cams—she's got this intensity about her that's coming from those letters. It's in the way she holds them close to her body, like they're a part of her somehow. I haven't seen that from her before, and I'm not sure what it means and I'm not even sure that it matters.

Still. That intensity. It's there.

FORTY-ONE

CAMILA

THE NEXT DAY, after lunch, my hands are shaking, but I'm determined to go through with it. As soon as I catch sight of Yolanda sitting alone, having handed out all the meds, I walk over to her. Stand awkwardly until I get her attention.

"Hi, Camila," she says. "How's it going?"

"Dr. Roberts said I could use the computer room until one today. I'm supposed to email my teachers about independent learning and summer school."

"Sure. That's fine. Make sure to check in with the aide there."

I remain standing there.

"Is there something else?" she asks.

"Well, I ran something by Dr. R in session, and she said to ask you about it. It's about dancing."

"What about dancing?"

"I was wondering if I could lead a dance class. Just a simple beginners thing. Like a workshop. I've been using the yoga studio for the last week or so, and I thought it would be cool to be able to offer a class to anyone else who would be interested."

Yolanda leans back, as if trying to get a better look at me. "You'd really want to do something like that?"

I shrug. "Yeah."

"You know, that makes me incredibly happy to hear," she says.

"It does?" My cheeks warm. "It's not that big a deal."

"It is a big deal," she insists. "This is what we mean when we talk about community building."

"Maybe," I say, although honestly, I'm just doing this for myself. Something in me craves creation. A sense of accomplishment. And after talking with those girls yesterday, this felt like a thing I could actually get off the ground. If I were allowed to.

"When do you want to do this?"

I shrug. "As soon as possible. Just on a trial basis, you know. I don't know if anyone would show."

"And you said you spoke with Dr. Roberts? What about your parents?"

"What about them?"

"I think we should ask them first and get their input."

My heart sinks. "Are you serious? They'll never let me."

"I'll call them."

"They'll just say no. It's too scary to let me do something. Better to keep me locked in a cage."

"You're not in a cage, Camila. Let me check on this. I'll get back to you."

"Great," I say. "Just what I wanted to hear."

I'm bristling with rage as I march toward the library. It's like this place is meant to make me crazy. All the things I love and long to do—well, I'm told they're not safe. And all the things that make me feel safe, like free will and independent thinking and personal space—those will harm me.

What's the point of it all?

What's the point of anything?

Thankfully the library's empty. I can't deal with talking to anyone at the moment, and I slouch in front of one of the computers with a grunt before pulling the bundle of music-box letters from the small tote bag I'm allowed to carry and setting them on the table beside me. Screw contacting my teachers back home. I'm here to do research on what I'm interested in.

The first thing I do, however, is pull up my email like a sadist. Not a lot's in there except one nice message from Ivan and also two responses from places I'd contacted about funding. Both places sound really happy that I'd reached out, and they're asking for more information on how they can help me realize my dream.

For a moment, I feel dizzy, detached, as if I'm actually leaving my body, but I force myself to close my eyes and focus on the breathing exercises Dr. Roberts taught me. I breathe and I breathe and let myself feel whatever I need to feel about this moment. Which is mostly fury. Despair. Utter helplessness.

But before long, another feeling bubbles to the surface, swimming around with all the rest. It's a little bit of pride, I think. With a hint of righteousness. Or maybe that's just what other people call bittersweet. Because my email pleas worked even if my plan to go to Fieldbrook didn't. There are people out there willing to care about strangers. About dance. And this helps me focus on what I really came here to do, which is to figure out who wrote the letters we found.

Backing out of my email, I pull up the search engine and stare at it. The hardest thing is not knowing *when* the letters were written. Yolanda told us patient records were kept for a maximum of seven years and the same was true for personal belongings. However, the amount of crap piled in that room—including some of the movies and books I'd spotted—made it seem like it'd been a lot longer since anyone cleaned the place out, so I work under the assumption the letters were written in the last ten years.

Pulling the first few letters from the envelopes, I scour the writer's words again. Dani and I finished reading them last night in our room, and the most frustrating thing is how abruptly the letters end. The girl, K, continued to write to her friend Mikell while referencing what we assume is her older brother's death in circumstances that aren't exactly clear. She also persisted in raging against her parents for their denial of their children's issues and the facility itself for trying to make her conform to their idea of "normal" rather than admitting it was the world that was broken and damaged and traumatizing.

I guess that's the part I relate to. Being fed the lie that taking meds and "doing the work" is always the answer, even when it's no different having a doctor prescribe aspirin because someone's hitting you over the head with a hammer. Or worse, you're told the only true path to healing is replacing that hammer with a pile driver. The whole process is backward and infuriating, and so I long to join K's revolution. To be the rebel I've never been willing to fight to be.

Leaning forward, I type in the obvious search terms, like "Mikell" and "butterflies" and also "Carson and Valerie twins." Only, nothing comes up. I pull at the bandage on my arm while I scan the letters again, and then I see it. It's not related to K, exactly, but it might help.

In the search bar, I type: "Georgetown," "meningitis," and "death."

The hits pop up immediately. News article after news article about a tragedy that played out in one of the freshman dorms at the famed campus. Six students were sickened in mid-November, and sadly, two died. Both were girls: Valerie Mendelsohn and Sally Samaras. The press photos are heartbreaking—they're just so young and alive. Like any girl I'd see in the hallway at my school. No doubt they were the pride of their families, going off to such an esteemed institution, only to be cut down in their prime. They were only eighteen.

I check the dates on the articles. They all ran in November of 2000, so nineteen years prior, which—if K's roommate was sent to Peach Tree Hills in the immediate aftermath of her sister's death—would indicate K was likely here at some point in 2001. Meaning, she's in her mid-thirties at this point.

That can't be right.

More searching. I'm able to pull up the obituaries for each girl. Sally's the only one who is referenced as having been survived by a younger sister, Chloe. So I type in the search bar: Chloe Samaras.

And then there she is. I suck in air. Thank God for uncommon names. Chloe's photos are less vibrant than Sally's—she comes off as the more serious sibling, although maybe this wasn't always the case. The resemblance between the two is evident.

Chloe and Sally both have the same high cheekbones, thick glossy hair, and dimpled chins.

A little more digging and I unearth Chloe's faculty profile on the website of a small private college in Colorado. It appears she's earned a PhD in Middle Eastern studies and has written a book on the Arab Spring. Her page has links to a couple of online interviews, but they're all focused on her scholarly work. None ask questions about her dead sister or the time she spent locked in a psychiatric facility.

"Hey," a voice behind me says.

I whirl around to see Dr. Sánchez standing in the doorway.

"Yeah?" I say.

"You're late for your therapy appointment." She points to the clock, and I don't know where the time went, but yeah, I'm ten minutes late.

"Sorry," I say. "I lost track of time."

"I thought we'd emphasized the importance of being where you're supposed to be."

"You did. I said I was sorry."

"Well, I'm not the one you need to apologize to," she says.

I duck my head, grab my stuff.

"Hold on."

I look at her.

She takes a step inside the library, clasps her hands in front of her. "Your parents. I called them earlier. Yolanda asked me to with regard to this dance class you're interested in teaching."

"You called them already?" I ask.

"Don't you want to know what they said?"

I sling the tote bag over my shoulder. "I don't know. Do I?"

Dr. Sánchez smiles. "I think so. They said yes."

I brighten. "Really?"

"Really. The only caveat is that you talk with them on the phone beforehand so that they understand what you're hoping to achieve by teaching this class."

"No. No way." I shake my head vigorously.

"It's just a brief call. That's it."

"No," I tell her. "It's never just one thing. They took some-thing from me, and they don't get to be the ones who give it back."

FORTY-TWO

DANI

"WHAT DID YOU MEAN," I ask Dr. Allegheny, "when you said Camila and I might not be all that different from each other?"

"When did I say that?"

"The last time we met. Right at the end. I said she was mad at me, and you said we might have something in common."

"Is something about that comment bothering you?"

"It's not bothering me. I just don't think I'm very much like Camila at all. I've been thinking lately that she reminds me a lot of my ex-boyfriend. They're both quiet and repressed, and they're both into self-harming or whatever."

"Your boyfriend?"

"Ex-boyfriend. And yeah, he had a thing with making weight for wrestling. But also, he's always been pretty . . ."

"Uptight?" Dr. Allegheny offers.

"I was going to say *unhappy*. But the point is that he and Camila are alike in a lot of ways, and I don't think I'm like either of them. They're both so sensitive. It's like they were born to suffer, you know?"

He nods. "I think I understand what you're saying. But from my recollection, when I compared you and Camila, I wasn't referring to your temperament or personality. It was in reference to her being angry at you for telling her doctor about the fact that she'd cut herself."

"Oh." I take this in. "Well, she's not mad at me anymore. We talked about it."

"I'm glad to hear that."

"I still don't get the comparison, though."

"Why don't you keep thinking on it," he urges.

"Sounds like you don't know the answer, either."

"Or maybe I just believe you do."

I'm five minutes late meeting up with Camila and Yolanda at the lost and found, and we're supposed to actually do some work today. I apologize when I reach them, but they barely acknowledge me.

"Do you have the key?" I ask breathlessly.

Camila holds it up, Yolanda waves goodbye, says she'll check in on us soon, and we start the walk across the courtyard toward the back meadow.

"You two look pretty friendly today," I say.

Camila shrugs. "I guess. We were just talking."

"About the letters?"

"About the dance class."

"Are you going to do it?"

"I want to. But on my terms."

"It will be on your terms. Whatever you decide," I say.

"We'll see." She sighs. "Oh, and she didn't know anything about the letters. I don't think she's asked yet."

"Have you heard from Chloe?" I venture because I know Camila's emailed her, even though she hasn't told me what the message said.

She shakes her head, walking to the locked door and sticking the key in. "Not yet. I'll check again later."

"I could write to her, too," I offer. "I like talking to people."

"We probably shouldn't overwhelm her." Camila shoves the door open, and I step in after her, switching on the overhead light. God, the place is still such a mess. Looking at it makes me want to lie down and go to sleep. Cams is more motivated, apparently. She starts whistling and goes right for the trash can, dragging it down one of the aisles. Then she starts pulling some of the older boxes of tapes and books down, organizing them into piles that mystify me.

I watch her for a moment, resisting the easy momentum of jumping in and helping, because something still feels off to me. It's hard to define. But it's not just that Camila wants to find the person who wrote the music-box letters and that she's being protective about this Chloe person. *I* want to find the letter writer, too. Hell, I love a good mystery. I guess it's just, with how angry she's been at her parents lately, and how little she believes in herself, I kind of wonder what Cams is *hoping* to find. K's happy ending?

Or something else?

FORTY-THREE

CAMILA

OKAY, I WASN'T totally honest with Dani. The truth is that I haven't sent an email to Chloe yet. I said I would, and I want to. But I want to say the right things. In the right way. So finally, after we work in the lost and found, I try again.

Dani has an art class, and late afternoon means the library's full of girls studying. Still, the aide there welcomes me in and reminds me that I can only be online for twenty minutes max. I thank him, and when I'm in my seat, I move quickly, typing the name Chloe Samaras into the search bar and again pulling up the woman's faculty profile. The link to her work email is there, and while holding my breath and telling myself to be brave, I click it. A text box pops up, and I start writing the message I've been composing in my head for the past two days. No one around here understands me. For some reason, I feel like Chloe might.

She *has* to.

Hi, Dr. Samaras,

My name's Camila, and I'm currently staying at a residential facility called Peach Tree Hills in Georgia. It's for girls dealing with mental health stuff like trauma and self-harm. Well, you don't have to tell me anything if you don't want to because I know this kind of stuff is supposed to be private or confidential or whatever, which I really respect. But my roommate and I found some old letters hidden inside a music box that were written a long time ago by a girl who was here. She mentioned that her roommate was someone we think was you. We want to find this girl and give her back the letters and the music box, and we also want to find out what happened to her.

I know it might seem silly or whatever to chase something like this, but it would be nice to know how someone who sounds a lot like me might've grown up.

Thank you.

Sincerely,

Camila Ortiz

I step outside, and I realize I'm smiling. That felt good, actually. I'd forgotten that hope can be something you create on your own.

This gives me another idea. I turn and walk to the main admin building, going all the way around the front to enter the reception area.

The woman at the desk looks up. "How can I help you, Camila?"

"I'd like to call my parents," I say, and before I know it, the phone's in my hand and I can hear the line ringing.

"Hello?" It's my father's voice, weary as always.

"Daddy," I say. "It's me, Cams."

FORTY-FOUR

DANI

IT TAKES A FULL WEEK, but Camila and I finally finish cleaning out the lost and found. My assumption's that Yolanda will assign us some other shit chore that she doesn't want to do, but it's like her anger's evaporated with the passage of time. She's too excited by the success of Camila's dance class—they're planning on making it a regular thing now—and it just feels as if everyone's moved on.

Except me.

"I'm tired," I tell Dr. Allegheny. "Nothing bad's happening, but none of it feels good."

"Tell me more about that," he says.

"It's just everyone around me—they're all participating in

the same activities that I am. Art therapy. Gardening. Group. Now Cams is teaching dance or whatever. But they're all into the things they're doing. Or they're pretending they are, and I just don't feel what they do."

"So you feel as if their participation isn't sincere?"

"I do feel that way. But what's that thing you always say?"

"About what?"

"That I'm not a mind reader. That I can't really know anyone else's intentions or motives. But yeah, to me their happiness comes off as insincere, but I don't have evidence of that. It's just how I feel."

"Feelings are emotions. So what emotion does their happiness evoke in you?"

"Irritation."

"At?"

I shake my head. "I know what I'm supposed to say. That *I'm* the problem. But that's not how I feel. To me, they're all fake. They're all just pretending because they don't know what else to do and they can't bear to accept that nothing about being here is meaningful."

"And this impacts you how?"

"It makes me feel crazy! Because either everyone else is easily fooled and therefore I can't respect them, or else they're willing to throw away their individuality and everything they believe in just for the comfort of conformity. Or . . ."

"Or what?"

"Or I *am* the problem. I'm the one who's wrong. It's like that movie. *In the Mouth of Madness.* Have you seen it?"

Dr. Allegheny shakes his head.

"Well, there's this guy who believes there's a disease infecting people and making them psychotic. But by the time he discovers that everyone on earth is infected, it dawns on him that he's actually the sick one."

"Are you worried you might be sick? Or psychotic?"

I lower my voice in dramatic fashion. "I'm worried that if I were, I wouldn't *know*."

Dr. Allegheny nods. "I see."

"Do you?"

"Absolutely."

"Then how do I fix it?"

"What do you want to fix?"

"Feeling this way! Like, I don't understand why I can't be like everyone else and just do all the feel-good things and be happy and enjoy conformity like the rest of the world."

"Maybe this is the time we talk more about your mother and you and your relationship to being Black."

I sneer. "What does *that* have to do with anything?"

"Well, you've mentioned living in an extremely wealthy white suburb in Dallas, right? And how your mother's image is the most important thing to her. So important that you feel as if she'd rather hurt you or suppress your individuality in order to preserve that image."

"That's true."

"Do you think there's a connection there to how you're feeling now?"

I lean back. "I don't understand what you're saying."

"Well, from what you've described, your mother's family's whole legacy has been built around proving that they can be just as successful as white folks."

"Right."

"So what do you think her standard of success looks like?" Dr. Allegheny asks.

"A rich white guy? Preferably one with a private jet. Or a small island somewhere."

"And what are the implications of that?"

"I mean, I have no clue. There's no winning for her there. Identifying with the oppressor and all that. But come on, she's a grown adult, and she's not gullible about the world we live in. It's not like she's begging racists for votes. She's all about Black society, but what I see as elitism, she sees as pride."

"What do you think that's like for her?"

My nose wrinkles. "I don't know. I need to think about that. I don't feel sorry for her, though. I'm allowed to have my own opinions."

Dr. Allegheny shifts in his seat. "Do you remember when

you told me that the reason you liked breaking rules and pushing boundaries was because it gave you a sense of control? That you were in charge of your own destiny?"

"Yeah."

"Do you think part of that control comes from rejecting your mother's process? One that, in your mind, emulates white supremacy in spite of contributing to her success as a Black woman?"

"Maybe. I could see that, I guess."

"Because if this is a dynamic that you've gotten into with your mother—rejecting what she values as your own way of self-preservation, then perhaps what's going on now is that you've somehow internalized all conformity with a loss of power. Not just the power struggle you have with your mom."

I press my fingers to my forehead. "I don't know. This is a lot to think about."

"It is a lot. But these are the issues we need to keep coming back to, because if you continue this pattern of rejecting all connection with other people in order to feel in control, then where does that leave you?"

"Here," I tell him. "In your office."

Dr. Allegheny smiles. "Touché. But, Dani, I do hear you saying how much you value your independence. And I also think that you're a good friend. You care deeply about other people, and so even though this work is hard, it's worthwhile. Because right now it feels as if being alone is proof of your freedom. But at the same time, I hear you saying it's *lonely*. And loneliness hurts."

"Yeah," I say. "It really, really does."

That night, after the nurse brings her meds, Camila heads for the shower.

"You staying up?" she asks me. "Some of the girls are watching a movie later."

"What movie?"

"I don't know. Something with magic. A fantasy."

"Are there babies born on fur?"

"What?"

"I won't watch anything that takes place in a pretend world where a baby might be born on fur. Real-world fur's okay."

"You're really weird," she says. "I'm leaving."

The door closes, and once she's gone, I don't know what to do with myself. With this low-level irritation that's grating at my gut. Plus it's hot. I pull my locs back off my neck, then pick at the zit on my nose, since my skin's an oily mess, and everything's just decided to be terrible, all at once. I bet Camila's taking one of her long showers, probably fantasizing about her precious class and how all the girls have been fawning over her lately. I mean, I'm happy for her.

Just not for me.

Then I do it. The thing I knew I would the instant she left tonight. I go to the closet, yank at the clothing rod, and slide out the pills I've hidden there. After opening the bottle, I tip one into my hand, a soft scored oval, and stare at it.

What would you do for me?

What do you have to offer?

The pill doesn't answer, and I hesitate, confused about what to do. About what rebellion even is anymore. Is it failing to prove to my mom that she's not perfect? Or is it succeeding in proving to her that I am?

Fuck.

Fuck.

FORTY-FIVE

CAMILA

THE SLIDING DOOR'S wide open, the sheer curtain flutter-
ing in the breeze, and right on the hour, the girls rush in. It's not
always the same eight, but the main core is unchanged. This is
more their space than mine, if you want to know the truth. They
made this happen, and I'm just one of the tools that helps give
them what they want.

"Come sit." I wave them over into a circle on the floor and
switch on some music—a classical Colombian piece that's all gui-
tar and heartbreak. "How's everyone doing?"

"Good," they tell me, and since this isn't therapy with
Dr. Roberts, I don't dwell on the question any longer than good

manners require. Besides, healing comes through movement. Expression, too.

"Let's warm up," I tell them, and they follow my cues, loosening up our muscles, getting into our bodies, and engaging in dynamic stretching in preparation for more. "I think you'll like what I've got for you today. We're going to try some choreography. All right?"

A hand goes up. "I've never done that."

"That's okay. I've never taught it, either. So it'll be a first for most of us. Are any of you K-pop fans?" A few girls nod. "Great. Then you might know this dance. It'll look hard when I first show it to you, but then we're going to break it down move by move. Although one thing—we'll isolate moves and work on them individually. But we don't ever slow down the move to learn it. You want to learn at the speed you'll be doing the move. In fact, it's better, ultimately, to get the timing down before anything else. Anyone know why?"

There are a number of blank looks or expressions that say: *I didn't know this was an academic class.* So I finally just answer, "Timing's the hardest part about dance. You lose that, it doesn't matter how pretty your moves are. The whole thing's ruined. Timing trumps all."

"Are you Korean?" a girl asks.

"What?"

"Is that where you're from?"

I sigh, and I mean, what do you do with that? I understand this girl is young, but damn, some people need to get out more and take a look at who's living in this country with them. "Well, my parents are originally from Colombia and Mexico, but I'm from right here in Georgia. Either way, I'm a long way from South Korea, but I love their music and what they're bringing to dance, especially the women. So let's get this started."

Dani's in a pissy mood when I get back to the room. I try telling her about the workshop and even suggest she comes to one, since I know she likes dancing, but she rebuffs me.

"So much for being selfish, huh?" she asks.

"What do you mean?"

"I mean, you're letting this place rope you into becoming a dance instructor for free. There's not really an upside for you, is there?"

"I don't mind. I like doing it. Besides, it was my idea, remember?"

"So maybe you *do* care what people think of you."

"How's that?"

"Well, you're making it sound like you're doing it just to be seen as altruistic."

"What's that supposed to mean?"

"I mean that if your supposed altruism is just virtue signaling for a boost in social currency, then maybe this whole thing is on brand for you."

I stare at her. "Why're you being such a bitch tonight?"

"I don't like hypocrisy."

"Well, I don't like knowing you stole pills from that house in Leeds, so I guess we're even."

"Fuck off," she snarls.

"Good night, Danielle." I shove my earplugs in and ready myself to crawl under the covers. "One of the benefits of not caring what other people think about me is that I have no problem ignoring you right now."

FORTY-SIX

DANI

I APOLOGIZE FIRST THING in the morning.

"It's fine," Cams says, but that's probably her selfishness talking—rejecting me as a way of keeping distance to avoid being hurt. Which is different than how I push people away by believing I'm too good for their friendship.

"No, really," I tell her. "I'm trying to not minimize other people's feelings. And that includes my own. It's a thing I do, I guess."

"What is?" She yawns, brushing her hair back before rubbing the sleep from her eyes.

"I avoid admitting I have feelings. I don't want other people to see anything vulnerable about me because then I'm not . . ."

"You're not what?"

"As in control as I thought I was."

"Where's this all coming from?" she asks.

"I'm just sick of being resentful all the time. I don't know why I feel this way, but I also don't know how to stop."

Camila yawns again.

"Maybe I'm just bored," I tell her. "Nothing ever happens here."

"I think that's the point. When stuff is happening, then you can avoid doing the hard stuff. You know?"

"Are you avoiding it?" I ask.

"I'm trying not to. Dr. Roberts says I put walls up as a way to avoid all the messiness of life. Which works. But it keeps out the good as much as the bad. So now I'm trying to lower the wall. A little bit at a time."

"Why?"

She gives me a pointed look. "Because messiness catches up to you one way or another."

"Is that the only reason?"

"I guess I'm just in the mood to try, you know?"

"I haven't taken any of the pills," I tell her.

"You shouldn't have them in the first place."

I nod. "Hey, that wall you mentioned . . ."

"What about it?"

"You talk about it like it's there to protect you. Like

that's the reason it exists. But what if it's built from something else?"

"Like what?" she asks.

I'm pensive. "Aggression. Or anger."

"You think I'm aggressive?"

"No," I admit. "But when you shut down, it can kind of feel that way. To me, at least."

Camila smiles.

"What's so funny?" I ask.

"Look at you, needing people. Caring about how they feel about you."

"Hush," I tell her.

But she keeps smiling.

Like Camila, I think I have to be willing to try. I tell myself this over the next couple of days as I move from therapy session to therapy session, as I fill out my thought logs and draw illustrations of my family tree and pluck weeds in the garden that sprout up after the afternoon rain and engage in discussions of racial injustice and the impact of generational trauma on collective well-being.

Still, there's nothing to do.

Still, nothing changes.

This includes, however, my continuing not to take any of the pills I stole from the house in Leeds.

So in a way, maybe something *is* changing. Maybe not doing something can be as powerful as doing it. Maybe, in life, all that really matters are the choices I make and who I choose to make them for.

"Come dance," Camila suggests for the millionth time, and after securing permission from the powers that be, I do. I do it more for her than for me. Camila's full of contradictions. For all she doesn't care about what other people think of her, she's cares deeply about her own standards. If I were to reject her, it might serve to reinforce her own inadequacy.

I don't want that burden. Also, if I'm being honest—which I'm making an effort to do more of these days—I kind of want to dance.

So I pull on some leggings and a tank top, and I head to the yoga studio.

I'm early, but Camila beams at the sight of me. "I'm so glad you're here!"

"Thought I'd check it out," I say, all casual, like I'm doing her the favor.

. "Well, look, we'll be going through some choreography that the other girls are somewhat familiar with, but I don't want you to feel nervous or anything. I'll help you and get you caught up real quick."

"Okay." My head tilts, but I do as she instructs and focus on not humiliating myself as the music comes on and I gamely follow along, sweat dripping down my back. This is a Camila I've never seen before. She's vibrant. Confident. And alive.

But me?

I'm here. I'm definitely here.

Only, I don't know what I am.

FORTY-SEVEN

CAMILA

I HUG DANI when the class is over, and I tell her how happy it made me to have her show up. She manages a smile and tells me I did a good job, but I can't help but sense there's something wrong.

"We're thinking of doing an actual performance next weekend," I tell her. "You should be a part of it. It'll be fun. I mean, you can tell—it's the other girls who are really running this whole thing, but it's been cool watching it come together."

"What's next weekend?" she asks.

"It's Family Day," I tell her. "There'll be a whole bunch of exhibitions that let our folks see what we've been up to and where their money goes."

"Oh, right." She wrinkles her nose. "Yeah, my parents

definitely aren't flying in from Texas to see some bullshit theater about how everyone's so happy and well-fed."

"Mine are coming," I say. Then: "It's obviously a lot closer for them. It's not a big deal or anything."

Her eyes narrow. "And you're okay with that? With seeing them?"

"I want to be. We've been talking a little bit with Dr. Roberts. Trying to fix our relationship."

"Jesus," she says bitterly. "Et tu, Camila?"

Once she's gone, I close up the studio and bolt for the library. I feel a pang of guilt; I always let the girls out early in order to check my email. This seems to call into question my dedication to their progress, but they haven't complained, and like my instructors always told me: It's better to end on a good note than a perfect one.

I slide into my corner desk and log on to the computer. The guilt's still there, stuck somewhere in my windpipe and tamping down any joy I might've felt while dancing. I should've been a better friend to Dani, but I can't fix her relationship with her parents. I'm having a hard enough time with my own.

I pull up my email account and smile when I see what I've been hoping for. A response from Chloe Samaras. *Finally.*

Okay, this will make Dani's day. I'm sure of it. But also, I get to read it first.

I kind of like that.

Hey, Camila,

Your letter was such a surprise! But a welcome one, and I'm glad to hear that you're working on whatever's going on in your life and trying to get better. None of those things are easy, and now that I'm older, I realize that most people don't ever do it. They don't self-reflect or grow or do much other than coast. That's because self-reflection is hard. It's often painful, but in my experience, it was so worth it. It's still worth it. It's not something you really ever finish. It's more of a journey you choose to take.

I'm afraid I don't have all the answers you're seeking. I'm not able to share my roommate's personal information because that's what privacy is: the right to choose when and with whom you share the most personal parts of yourself. I can't take that choice from her, but I can offer a little bit of insight that you might find helpful.

First of all, reading your letter, I was struck by how much you remind me of her, the girl you're calling "K." She, too, was always trying to figure out why the world worked the way it did. Nothing was ever left to fate, she liked to tell me. There was no such thing as destiny.

273

You know, it used to piss me off when she'd say that, considering how we lost my sister. *That* had happened without any warning. We got a call midday on a Tuesday that she was sick and heading to the school infirmary, and by eight p.m. she was gone.

The idea that her dying alone without her family was simply random and without purpose just about killed me. I couldn't stand it—the thought that if Sally had simply come home for the weekend instead of staying in the dorms or if she'd been transferred to the local hospital an hour earlier than she was that she might still be here. In my mind, *random* meant that the most earth-shattering and horrific event of my life was something that could be chalked up to bad luck, like stepping in gum or spilling food on your shirt.

I couldn't believe in a world that cold and empty. I didn't. And yet, that was the world I found myself in.

K was different, obviously. Now that I'm older, I can look back and see that my existential rage and grief were the product of what had been a pretty sheltered life. I genuinely expected life to be fair, and I didn't know then that meaning isn't something you're handed. It's what you make of tragedy. That *that's* the work we're all put on this earth to do.

But K came from a different background, and her

belief in the justness and rightness of anyone's existence had long been shattered. Still, that's a story for her tell. So with that, I wish you all the luck in finding her and all the best in finding yourself.

 —Chloe

FORTY-EIGHT

DANI

"HEY, DADDY," I say when he picks up.

"Dani!" he exclaims in his booming voice. "How are you, baby? Where are you?"

"Where do you think? I'm in Georgia. At the facility."

"It's so good to hear from you. Should I get your mom?"

"Hold on, Daddy," I tell him. "I can only talk for a minute. I wanted to ask you something."

"How are things? Are you doing what you're supposed to?"

"I'm trying. I'm doing a lot of therapy, and I think that's going well even if it sucks sometimes. My shrink is helping me find new coping skills and also to understand myself and why I have a hard time connecting with people. He says I hate conformity so much, I don't let myself have a community."

"Did you hear your mom won reelection?"

I grip the phone. "No. That's great. Look, Daddy, can I ask you something?"

"Sure, baby. What is it?"

"I know it's short notice, but this weekend we're having a Family Day of some sort. I'll be in a dance performance. I know you're far away, but it'd be great if you came."

"Your mother and I? You want us there?"

"If you can."

"I don't know her schedule, baby. I'll check. She's been busy."

"That's fine. I just thought I'd ask. I can ask Aunt Bea, too."

"Oh, that's a great idea! She's so much closer. Damn it, hold on. I think the caterer's here. Can you wait a minute? I'm going to put the phone down."

"No, Daddy, it's fine. I'll let you go."

"You sure? I can try and find your mom. She's around here somewhere."

"No, it's good. Don't go to any trouble. I love you, Daddy."

"Bye, baby," he says. "Thanks for the call."

Tears well up in my eyes after I hang up the phone and I thank the residential aide, handing her the phone back, before turning and running outside, heading for the pond. I'm supposed to be at gardening, and Yolanda's going to send a search party if I'm not there in like two minutes, but I don't care. Let them kick me out. Let me be my parents' problem again so they can see how much they like it.

They would deserve it, having me come home only to raise more hell. My mom especially. I used to love dressing up for photo shoots or getting my hair done with her and tagging along to all her events. It felt so special. Like no one could touch us. But the minute I questioned her means—not even her motives—she turned on me. And sure, maybe Dr. A's right that's she's got her own shit to deal with, but I'm her *kid*. It's not up to me to fix her. It's up to her to love me.

But I don't know that she does.

"Danielle! Danielle!" I turn and see a group of girls standing lined up in the grass. One of them's waving at me.

"What is it?" I call.

"We're practicing."

"Practicing what?"

"The dance!" The girls look impatient. "Come on. You want to join us?"

"I'm supposed to be in the garden."

"We all are. Yolanda said we can practice, though."

Interesting. "Where's Camila?" I ask.

"She's working on her solo."

"A solo?"

"It's a surprise! Don't tell her we told you. But we want to be ready for Saturday. You're going to be there, right?"

"I guess," I say. "As far as I know."

The girls grin. "Come on, then! Let's make her proud."

I turn and look back at the dorm, to where the pills are. They could be my ticket home. My ticket to not giving a fuck ever again about anything. But it would be a whole fight to get into my room right now. I'd have to do a bunch of lying and hope Yolanda doesn't catch me first. Then I turn and look back at the waving girls, the ones who want me to join them and dance and be a part of their fun.

So I do.

Join them.

PART III:

WHEN WE LEARNED TO SAVE OURSELVES

FORTY-NINE

CAMILA

A CHANGE—I'm the one who wakes up early. It's Saturday morning, and it's not the dance exhibition, or even the solo I've been practicing, that's putting me on edge. It's my *parents*. I glance at the window, hints of sunshine already pushing through the pale curtains, and it's hard to know how to parse the feelings that are coursing through me.

There's still so much rage and remorse wrapped up in what's happened. Wrapped up in how I feel about them. I know they never wanted to hurt me, but this is almost the most infuriating part because saying that is like saying I don't deserve my anger. Like I'm a bad person for resenting their love and how scared they were when I hurt myself. But Dr. Roberts has been telling me my rage is a good thing. And that before coming here, I didn't know how to recognize my anger, and that this contributed to my suicide attempt. Because anger serves a purpose, she says. It helps you set boundaries and helps you survive. Trying to ignore or pretend it's not there isn't helpful.

In fact, it hurts.

I dig around in the dresser for the clothes I'm going to wear. Just boy shorts and a bra top. Because it's hot now! The mugginess has been gross, too. Obviously the bra top means the scars on my side will show, but for once, I'm okay with that. Everyone's already seen the wound on my arm, the one that got stitched, so what are a few more? Besides, a dancer doesn't hide her body, I've decided. It's part of the story, part of what makes dance art. And I love that. I always have. I just haven't always loved myself.

So now I'm trying.

Clothes in hand, I putter to the bathroom and step into the shower stream, relishing the cool water in the already-warm air. God, I wish I could know the future. That's what scares me most lately. There are definitely pockets of hope out there, especially when I think about teaching or working with kids one day. But I just want to know, for once, that things will be okay. Really okay. That no more trains of shit are waiting up ahead, stalled out on the tracks.

I also wish I could talk with K. I'd love to find out whether or not she still believes in destiny. Whether meaning and purpose ever ended up colliding with the events in her life. And if so, how did she get there?

Dani's still asleep when I return to our room. So I pounce on her bed, startling her awake.

"Get up!" I watch as her face moves from utter confusion to laughter. "It's time to wake up! My parents are coming!"

"God help us," she says.

I only get a chance to see them briefly before we have to set up for the dance exhibition. But the minute I spot my parents walking across the lawn, hand in hand, looking awkward and, frankly, terrified, I can't help myself. I run to them, hold them close.

My father clings to me in that way he does, and this is when I realize he's crying.

"Oh, Daddy," I say. "It's okay. I'm okay. I'm so happy you're here."

He nods, wipes his eyes, then excuses himself in search of the restroom. Once he's gone, my mom kisses my cheek, tucks my hair behind my ear. "He's missed you so much. I have, too, sweetie."

"I know," I say. "But being here, it's been good for me. It's helped a lot."

"I'm glad," she says.

"I'm teaching dance, you know."

"You told us. You have a whole class."

A surge of pride ripples through me. "Are you ready to see what I've been doing with them?"

She nods.

"Are you sure?" I ask, watching her reaction closely. Something in me needs to push a little. Not in an aggressive way, like Dani said, but in a wall-tearing-down way. In a way where I want my feelings to be acknowledged. "I know you think dancing isn't good for me."

"We never said that, Camila."

"You," I say. "I'm specifically talking about you right now. Not Daddy or anyone else. Stop trying to deflect blame for your choices."

She looks surprised. I've learned some new vocabulary at Peach Tree Hills. "I'm not deflecting."

"You are. And you didn't have to say it, you know. Not when you turned my admission offer down without telling me. I hated that, and I know that's hard for you to hear. But it's true."

Her lip trembles. "We— *I* did that because I was scared. I didn't know what to do or how to break it to you, and so I let your doctor tell you. That was cowardly. I know it was, and I'm sorry."

I soften. "Thank you."

"I want to see you dance. I always have. Your father, too."

"Well, good," I say. "I'm glad. That's a start."

I think have a grand total of twenty audience members, who all sit ringed around the edge of the dance studio. It's hardly a sellout crowd, and it's definitely not a true stage.

But it's the one we have.

Standing by the stereo, I look at the girls and ask, "Are you ready?"

When they say yes, I hit play. The music comes on, and the two formations begin striding toward each other, hands on their hips. I step back.

Watch.

And they're amazing.

They sell it with their energy—if not always the moves—and every time I glance at their parents, at the other girls, their expressions are rapt. Some of the girls clap along, and three minutes later, when it's over, everyone's cheering. Including me.

"You were so great," I tell them as we join in a bear hug of laughter and celebration. "I can't believe it."

"It's your turn now, right?" they ask. "You're going to dance for us, aren't you? That's what you said."

It is what I said, and I am nothing if not true to my word. I look at Dani, who knows what music to cue.

Clearing my throat, I stand in front of the audience and wait for the applause to die down. "Thank you. I've had such a wonderful time working with these amazing dancers. They've taught me so much more than I've taught them, and I just feel so grateful to have had this chance to work in an art form that has meant so much to me in my life. Before coming here, I thought dance was everything. And also that it was the only thing that could make me happy. So when it didn't, my life kind of fell apart. Over these last six weeks, however, I've been trying to put myself together again and find a way to connect with dance that isn't about escape or running away from feelings I don't like to have. So I wanted to dance for you now but also have it be a way of joining with you, not holding you at a distance."

And with that, I give a nod, Dani hits play, and I do it.

I dance.

FIFTY

DANI

LATER, AT THE MAIN parent reception on the lawn, everyone's milling around and drinking punch and eating cookies. Aunt Bea is talking with Dr. Sánchez, and I use the time to sneak away and find Camila, who's digging in a tub of ice for a soda. Diet Sprite, to be exact.

"You were so good!" I squeal, but in a quiet way since Yolanda just grabbed a microphone and appears to be getting ready to talk, and I know she'll give me that stink face if I so much as make a peep.

"Thanks," she whispers. All around us, the other girls are paired off with their parents, which makes for interesting people watching. "You guys were great, too. Where's your aunt?"

I point. "Over there, chatting up the boss."

Camila waves shyly at Aunt Bea. "I'm sorry your folks couldn't come."

I feel a pang but say, "Don't worry about it. It was a long way to fly for the weekend. Where are your parents?"

"Right there." Camila points out a couple standing near the cookie table. They're both tiny, like she is, with wide, worried eyes. "They didn't know about the dancing—my solo part—so I'll have to see how much it freaked them out. We've only been able to talk briefly. There's still a lot more to say."

"Will you introduce me later?" I ask.

She nods. "Of course."

With the mic, Yolanda starts to speak while waving her arms for everyone to look at her. "Good afternoon! Parents and family members, thank you for being here and for being a part of this event, which allows you to see some of the work your teens have been engaging in, as well as some of the fun and bonding that we do here.

"Right now, we thought it would be nice to hear from some of our alumni, who have varying degrees of distance from their own time here at Peach Tree Hills. We have two speakers today, who—I hope—have interesting personal stories about what role their stay here has played in their ongoing development and how it's impacted the course of their lives. I also hope that hearing from these speakers helps break down some of the barriers we have in our society in talking about mental health. The stigma itself can be damaging, which is why we value hearing from past residents."

"Always with the stigma," Cams whispers. "God, she's nothing if not predictable."

"Don't forget didactic."

"And sometimes mean."

I elbow her again, gently this time, but don't say anything else. I'm not sure *mean* is the word I'd use to describe Yolanda. More like strict or out of touch. She cares, though. I think that's real.

"Well, our first speaker tonight is kind of a surprise," Yolanda says. "Can anyone guess who it is?"

There's silence. I look around a bit and see if I can spot anyone. There's a woman I've never seen before holding an iced tea. She looks too young to be a parent, but I have no idea how to guess who she is.

"It's me," says Yolanda.

Cams pokes me. "Wait, what did she say?"

Yolanda continues. "That's right. I was a resident here at Peach Tree Hills quite a while ago. Almost twenty years, which is kind of surreal to consider. And I know that most of you think of me as the 'fun stopper,' since I'm in charge of day-to-day operations. But I do have some understanding of what it's like to be here and how scary and upsetting and unfair that can feel sometimes.

"So, this is my story. I haven't told it in a while, so I might be a little rusty with some of the details, but here goes. I grew up in Sarasota, Florida. I lived with both of my parents until they got divorced when I was eight. It was pretty terrible. They were very angry at each other, and I witnessed some violence in the home. After that, I lived primarily with my mother and stepfather in an area of the state known for sinkholes. They got married when I was ten, and at that point, I also had a stepbrother who was one year older than me, and twins—a boy and a girl—who were two years younger.

"The only one I got along with was the older brother. He played in a band and loved boats and was generally a kind person. Me, on the other hand, I was a really unhappy teenager. I pushed people away. Broke rules. Drank. Partied. I can't explain it except to say that I don't think I ever saw my life extending past my adolescence. When my mom would tell me to care about grades and college, it meant nothing to me because I wasn't going to be here to do any of that stuff that wasn't mine to have in the first place."

I bite my lip and sneak a glance at Camila, who's already looking at me with her eyes all wide. Yolanda, the bad girl? It's not something I can picture. At all.

"Anyway, when I was sixteen, the worst thing happened. My stepbrother was killed in a car accident leaving a party I'd taken him to. He was drunk, and everyone blamed me. I did, too, although I don't know why. I didn't make him drive or drink, but guilt was such a normal thing for me. It was like I was very powerful and also totally insignificant all at once."

This, I can picture. Not Yolanda, but what have I been doing my whole life if not trying to prove my power in the face of parents who refuse to accept it? Then I feel a pinch on my forearm. I look at Cams and see that every muscle in her body is tensed. Like a hunting dog.

"It wasn't much later that I tried to kill myself," Yolanda says. "I was in a relationship with one of John's bandmates, and he felt guilty the way I did, too. We had this plan to take pills and drink and lie down on the beach on the Gulf shore and wait for God to take us home. Only, Mikell freaked out and called for an ambulance before that could happen. We both ended up at the hospital, and then I ended up here."

Now I'm doing the pinching.

"Mikell?" I mouth to Camila.

She nods. Yolanda continues to talk about her time at Peach Tree Hills as a teenager. She doesn't mention her roommate by name but does reference living with a girl who was also grieving but who dealt with it in a very different way than she did. Somehow their differences and their vulnerabilities were what brought them together and out of their own tragedies.

Just like me and Camila.

When she's done speaking, everyone claps, and I swear she

looks right at Camila and me, like she knows what we're thinking about her. But it's not until after the next speaker is finished and we break for dessert that we're able to run over to her.

"You wrote those letters?" Camila asks.

"I'm glad you found them." Yolanda smiles knowingly.

"You put them there for us to find?"

"I did."

"So that's why you had us clean out that room," I say. "It wasn't punishment, was it? You wanted us to bond."

"I'll let you interpret that chain of events as you wish."

"Why did you sign the letters K?" Camila's got these little worry lines around her lips. Like all these details are super important to her.

"It was short for a nickname Mikell gave me."

"What was it?"

"Kryptonite. As in I was his." She blushes. "There was a silly song about it at the time, and we were young and very angsty."

"I like it," I say definitively.

"I'm glad. And I'm glad the letters were finally opened. I wrote them not knowing his current address and figured I'd send them eventually. But that didn't happen."

"Where he is now?" Camila asks.

"Working for his daddy in Boca."

"And you ended up here."

"I did. When I first left, I went back home and realized

it wasn't a healthy place for me to be. And being with Mikell wasn't, either, although I still cared for him. I still do, actually. We're friends. Well, friendly, at least. I ended up working my way through community college. Then I got a scholarship to UF, and after a lot of hard work, here I am."

"Good for you," I say.

"It's a hard job. But I love it."

"The strangest thing," I tell her, "is that I believe you."

She laughs. "I'm glad."

"The music box," Camila blurts out. "Is that yours?"

Yolanda shakes her head. "It was actually my roommate's. She was a dancer for a long time, but she left it behind when she went home. We used to wind it up and listen to the music at night, so I always thought she wanted me to still be able to do that when she was gone. I meant to give it back, but we lost touch over the years, and so using it for the unsent letters just felt right."

Camila beams. "I agree."

"It might be time for it to return to its rightful owner, how-ever. Do you want to give it to her?"

She blinks. "Give who what?"

Yolanda laughs. "The music box. To my roommate. I think you've corresponded with her."

This is when a tall blond woman walks over, puts her arm around Yolanda's shoulder. "I'm Chloe. You must be Camila?"

Camila's jaw completely drops. "You're here?"

The woman beams. "I loved your solo piece. You're very talented."

"Wait. I can't believe this," Cams says. It's like she's meeting someone famous. "You're a dancer?"

"I was in my younger years. Now I'm more into snowboarding. But you really did a great job with your performance today, and I loved what you said about your connection to dance. Thank you."

"You're welcome. I mean thank you. For the compliment," Camila says.

"And, Chloe, this is Danielle," Yolanda says. "She's Camila's roommate. They've been working together to find both of us."

"It's very cool to meet you," I say. Playing it much cooler than Cams, if I do say so myself.

Chloe grins. "The feeling's mutual. Believe me."

SIX MONTHS LATER

DANI

I LEAVE AS SOON as I get the call. Aunt Bea's kind enough to drive me since I don't have my Georgia license yet. I don't need it in Atlanta. The new school I'm going to is right on the bus line, and the city's easier to explore on foot.

I also feel safer that way. More grounded. Texas has such a vastness to it that I both love and know is capable of swallowing me whole.

So walking it is.

"When did it happen?" my aunt asks me because I haven't shared the details with her yet. She just knew it was important and she dropped everything to bring me, and for that I am so, so grateful. It's been an adjustment, living with Aunt Bea. She's particular about things like noise and food and what time I go to bed and who I'm hanging out with and if I've started on my college essays yet (I have!).

But also, she trusts me.

I tug at my seat belt and stare at the racing landscape, all those trees and rolling hills. Everything comes rushing back to me—the memory of riding out here that first time, having come so close to hitting a real rock bottom without even knowing it. Having flirted with my own destruction in search of proof that I was alive and that I could make change in my world. It wasn't until that last session with Dr. Allegheny that I really put all the pieces together.

It was also when I handed him the bottle of pills.

"What's this?" he asked me.

"Something I don't need. Or want."

"Was it from that house?"

"Yeah. You should've searched me when I got back. In addition to doing the drug tests. Although I never took any. It's a full bottle. Thirty pills. You can count."

"I appreciate you bringing these in. I know that must've been a hard decision."

"It's not hard," I say. "That's kind of the point and why I feel okay leaving. So thank you."

"You're welcome."

"By the way, I get it now," I told him.

"Get what?"

"What you tried to tell me after that stunt we pulled in

Leeds. You tried to tell me we're similar, Camila and I, because after she hurt herself, I said partying was my way of creating a reality that I could control. Even if that control was an illusion, it was my illusion. And that's what makes addiction so fucking hard to quit. It's *yours*. And if nothing else is, who would give that up?"

Dr. Allegheny smiled. "How do you feel about the comparison now?"

"Sad," I said.

"How so?"

"Because I understand. I get that her cutting was no different than what I was doing, even if I couldn't see that then. But that's what you were saying. You were telling me that drinking and doing drugs and pretending I could exist outside the complicated bullshit of reality was its own form of self-harm. Meanwhile, I was telling myself my actions were something other than what they were—like control or rebellion or agency. But they weren't. There were just a way to hurt myself when I didn't know what else to do."

"So what are you sad about?"

"Everything. I'm sad that sobriety means accepting that my parents can't be there for me in the way that I need them to. In the way that I even think they want to, which is the saddest thing of all. But sobriety and acceptance both feel honest, and so I'll take sad any day if that's what it takes."

"You're a smart young woman, Danielle."

I laughed. "Tell me something I don't know."

"Is there anything else on your mind?"

I shrug. "I guess I'm sad for Camila, too."

"Why?"

"Because I don't think she gets it yet. In her heart. She wants to, but I don't think . . ."

"You don't think what?"

I sigh. "She's delicate, you know? Like a butterfly. Or maybe the world's just too cruel for someone like her."

Now, outside the window, Leeds whips by, the green, the town square, the cobblestone walkways. It's autumn now, and the trees are turning, and I can't help but wonder where the students are. In school, I guess, although it's possible Christian's finally made his way to Stanford to bask in all their ~~liberal~~ capitalist glory.

"Here we are." My aunt pulls into the familiar driveway, typing in the gate code and easing her car along the gravel to park in the designated visitors area. Stepping into the frigid air, I'm awash in sudden foreboding. Together we stand in the shadow of the admin building, staring up at its thick Greek columns and looming archway.

I don't want to be here, I tell myself.

I never wanted to come back.

Not like this.

"You ready to go in?" my aunt asks. I nod, and she takes my hand, squeezing it as we walk up the stairs and through the front door.

"Danielle!" It's Dr. Roberts. She's waiting for us. Dr. Sánchez, too. They both hug me, pulling me close and thanking me for making the trip.

"Of course," I say. "What happened?"

"We don't know too much right now. Just that her parents said she's been struggling lately. She's been withdrawn. Isolating. Not even getting up for her classes—dance or otherwise. And then . . ."

And then.

"Yeah," I say.

"Have you been in contact with her?"

"We text all the time. She even came down to Atlanta last month and told me about the class she was teaching. I thought everything was good." My eyes start to sting. "I don't get it."

Dr. Roberts hands me a tissue and pats my shoulder in that shrinky way they all do. "I know. But recovery's rarely a straight line. It's a journey. And she's here, okay? She's safe."

"Can I see her?" I ask.

"Of course. She just got here this morning, and she's in one of the intake rooms."

"Does she know I'm coming?"

She shakes her head. "I didn't want to get her hopes up."

"Where's Yolanda?"

"You didn't hear? She went back to school this fall to get her doctorate. She keeps in touch, though. I'll tell her you say hi."

"Thanks." I try to hide how disappointed I am. Somehow I think seeing Yolanda right now might make me strong enough to do what I have to do. But suddenly I can hear Yolanda's voice, clear as day, telling me I need to find that strength within myself to be the friend who stays, even for the hard parts.

"Here's her room." Dr. Roberts knocks, then opens the door and smiles. "Camila, there's someone here to see you."

I pause, uncertain. My mind spins back through the all the texts we've shared since leaving. What did I miss? What didn't I want to see? She'd actually written to me two nights ago, and it'd felt like we were closer than ever. To each other. To our dreams.

Hey, she'd said. *You around?*

Me: *Of course. What's up?*

Her: *Nothing! I was just thinking about that time you stole the bed by the window. That was when I knew we'd be friends. Well, I didn't know that exactly. But I was intrigued. I wanted to know who you were.*

Me: *I stole a bed?*

Her: *Only because I let you. But, like, you had the nerve to ask for what you wanted. To think you deserved it.*

Me: *I think that's called entitlement, babe. Not my best quality.*

Her: *Maybe. For some people, sure. But not you, and for me, at that moment, I kinda needed to see that. That there are different ways to be in this world.*

Me: *You want to know what moment I remember?*

Her: *What's that?*

Me: *When you told me to back off making fun of Tess and her conspiracy theories.*

Her: *I told you that?*

Me: *Not in so many words, but yeah. You have a way of seeing the tenderness in people. Myself included.*

Her: *How's school? Are those APs kicking your butt?*

Me: *School's good! I kind of miss not being in Texas for my senior year. It's a weird feeling not finishing something I started so long ago.*

Her: *I get it. You're doing great, though. And now I better go. It's late! But I just wanted to tell you I was thinking about you. That I think about you a lot and all the time we spent together.*

"Dani?"

I hear her voice, and suddenly my hesitation is gone. I walk into the room, and I go straight to her. Camila lies in the bed, awake but groggy, and the fuzziness in her expression tells me the sedatives they have her on must be strong. The bandages on her wrists also tell me those sedatives are needed, and I have to hope she's not in too much pain. Dr. Roberts brings me a chair. I thank her and take it gratefully, pulling myself up to Camila's bedside.

"You're here," she says, her eyes filling with tears. "You came. Thank you."

"Oh, Cams." I lean closer, and while I don't know what to say or how to make things better, I don't let that stop me. I murmur in her ear how happy I am to see her and how, since our last conversation, I've also been thinking a lot about our time at Peach Tree Hills. About what it was like to first come here. Originally, I tell her, I'd only agreed to come out of anger and spite and a desire to prove my mother wrong in how she judged me and looked down on my choices. I'd also convinced myself that running away would show her how deeply her choices were hurting me. In my mind, the only thing that mattered was getting her to admit her failures—both as a parent and a politician. And while Dr. Allegheny helped me process this, Camila was really the one who helped me to see there was more to life than my petty grievances and the urge for rebellion. Who showed me the ways in which addiction and depression are both well-versed in lies, so eager to dress up self-destruction as the one true path toward freedom.

But it was hard being here, I tell her. A lot of it sucked, and it was genuinely one of the hardest experiences I've ever been through. But I couldn't have done it without her, I say, and I want her to know how strong and perfect I think she is. How strong and perfect she'll always be. The friendship between us is different and far more real than any I've ever had before, and for that I am so very grateful. And yeah, sure, I know she's probably internally rolling her eyes at my sappy "the friends we made along the way" sentiment. But she's changed me, I tell her, and change is a funny thing. It rarely happens because we want it to, and often in spite of what we think we need. Regardless, every minute I've been lucky enough to spend with Camila has felt like a miracle.

Like a goddamn gift.

When I look again, Camila's dozed off—her eyelids shut, her jaw slack. I sit and watch the rise and fall of her chest, the soft curve of her chin. Then I reach to brush the hair from her temple.

"Fight on," I whisper. "You're not alone."

ACKNOWLEDGMENTS

Many thanks to everyone who helped to make this book a reality during a time when reality was shifting and changing into something unrecognizable and unknown. Fiction has felt different during the pandemic—both writing and reading it. Common touchpoints are gone, as is any sense of certainty that the world I'm striving to create on the page reflects the one we live in.

I especially want to thank my editor Kieran Viola, for all of her kindness and wisdom. Thank you also to Cassidy Leyendecker, Zareen Johnson, Sara Liebling, Guy Cunningham, Mark Steven Long, Seale Ballenger, Dina Sherman, Holly Nagel, Andrew Sansone, Marybeth Tregarthen, and all the wonderful people at Hyperion who have worked so hard to bring this story to life. Thank you always to Michael Bourret and the fabulous crew at Dystel, Goderich & Bourret. Finally, thank you to my amazing family. Will, Sidney, Tessa, and Severin—you lift me up, and I love you more than anything.

RESOURCE LIST

National Suicide Prevention Hotline
https://suicidepreventionlifeline.org/
1-800-273-8255

NAMI Crisis Text Line
https://www.crisistextline.org
Text Hello to 741741

TeenTalk
https://teenlineonline.org/
CALL 1-800-852-8336
Text Teen to 839863

SMART Recovery Teen and Youth Support Program
Addiction Recovery Help for Teens and Young Adults
https://www.smartrecovery.org/teens/

To Write Love On Her Arms
https://twloha.com